THE TEXAN'S JOURNEY HOME

JOLENE NAVARRO

LOVE INSPIRED
INSPIRATIONAL ROMANCE

ISBN-13: 978-1-335-93167-2

The Texan's Journey Home

Recycling programs for this product may not exist in your area.

Love Inspired
22 Adelaide St. West, 41st Floor
Toronto, Ontario M5H 4E3, Canada
www.LoveInspired.com

MIX
Paper | Supporting responsible forestry
FSC® C021394

Printed in Lithuania

Strength and honour are her clothing;
and she shall rejoice in time to come.
—*Proverbs* 31:25

This book is dedicated to Jesus Alfredo "Fred" Navarro
for his persistent belief in me until I believed in myself.

Chapter One

Lyrissa rushed out of the crowded restroom as she dried her hands. She hadn't wanted to leave the boys alone for a second, but some things just couldn't be avoided. Especially after being in a car for more than twelve hours. They were back in Texas and so close to the ranch where she grew up. Port Del Mar might live too much on gossip for her liking, but her father's ranch was always safe.

They just had a few miles left and hopefully she wouldn't run into anyone. This new situation was going to have stories flying along the shoreline and her father didn't deserve any of it. Once again, the train wreck of a woman who called herself Lyrissa's mother had rammed straight into their lives without any thought of others. Deeann Herff Martinez had torn apart their family for the sake of finding her own happiness.

She pulled the scrunchie off her wrist and tried to wrestle her curls back into a ponytail. The humidity and coastal air were not her friend.

She hadn't wanted to waste time in front of a mirror with the boys waiting.

Buc-ee's was one of the best convenience stores in Texas, but still. She had told them if they stayed at the fudge counter then they would each get to pick a flavor when she returned. It was still hard to comprehend that she had two brothers, eight-and five years old. They were the only reason she had allowed her mother back into her life.

Of course, that had proven to be a huge mistake—not her brothers, but her mother. Dee was and would forever be a party girl first and foremost in search of an easy high. Why did Lyrissa think this time would be any different?

The sad part? At forty-five, Dee was still looking for the big score and next hit. This time, the woman had abandoned her two young sons and stolen everything of value from Lyrissa's apartment and wiped out her checking account. At least Dee hadn't been able to access Lyrissa's savings, not that it was much.

She was resigned to the fact that her mother would never change, and it would be up to her to make sure her brothers had a safe place to live.

Her neighbor had told her to call the police and turn the boys over to Child Protective Services, but she couldn't do that. The one time her mother had taken her when she had left the ranch, Lyrissa had ended up in the custody of CPS until her grandmother and father had been contacted. As a nine-year-old, she had been terrified that she would never see her father or grandmother again. She had just wanted to go home.

Her brothers didn't even have a home. But they had her now... She stopped. Where were they? Fear seized her lungs.

They were gone. Frantically scanning the large store again, she gazed from person to person and in between. The Texas-size truck stop was clean, well-lit and huge. It was filled with a mix of tourists and locals but there was no sign of the boys.

Had Bennett, the eight-year-old, taken his little brother back into the bathroom? *Breathe.* She needed to find an employee to check for her. As she leaned over the counter to get the attention of one of the candymakers, a gentle touch on the back of her shoulder caused her to jump.

"Ma'am?" A deep Texas drawl, cool and confident, ran along her nerves.

She turned and saw both boys. She took a deep breath with immediate relief. *They're safe.* She clenched her hands to her chest so she wouldn't grab her brothers and startle them.

They wouldn't appreciate the uninvited affection. Bennett had perfected the sullen look mixed with an air of boiling rage. Ray-Ray, younger by three years, was impossibly shy but wanted to trust her. He reminded her of a puppy that had been kicked too many times. The tears in his big brown eyes pulled pieces of her heart right off. His expression warned her that he could burst into sobs any minute.

"Lyrissa?" That voice.

Pull yourself together, girl. The question in the man's voice brought her gaze up to his. He was tall, dark and good-looking. Had to be a little over six feet. And well-built. His large hand gently sat on Bennett's shoulder. Not too tight, but firm enough to make sure the boy didn't run. His golden-brown eyes stared at her.

Reno Espinoza. Her heart sank. Of all the people to meet on this little side trip into town, why did it have to be him? When she had left Port Del Mar eight years ago, that had included standing him up for the homecoming dance. Had she at least sent him a text saying she couldn't make it? She hoped, but probably not. She had been humiliated and in too much of a rush to leave town.

Meeting his gaze, she expected judgment or resentment. But she only saw a genuine concern. The warmth and softness of his gaze was at odds with the hard jaw and wide mouth. Evidence of the Indigenous warriors who were his ancestors.

His thick, dark hair was a casually tossed mess, just like in high school.

With a sigh, she attempted a smile. He was one of the Espinoza kids. It was a well-known fact that they were the nicest family in town. Reno was the youngest and had the reputation of being the party boy, the one and only wild child of the bunch. He was famous for always wearing a smile and having fun in any situation. But that was when they were teenagers.

Reno was a grown man now, very grown. A loud rumble of thunder shook the building. Ray jumped and the older boy put an arm around him, pulling him closer. She needed to focus and get the boys to the ranch.

"Hey, Reno." She nodded, then looked back at her brother. "What's going on, Bennett? You were supposed to stay at the fudge counter. Both of you." Her gaze slid to Ray.

"He didn't mean it. Please don't get mad." Sweet Ray-Ray was already pleading for his brother.

Reno's eyes went wide for a second. "So, they *are* yours?" He looked at Bennett, doing the math. *Great.* She scanned the area. Rumors and stories, true or not, spread fast in these parts. Actually, the faster they flew, the further from the truth they grew.

Of course, when it came to her mother, there

had been more truth in the gossip than Lyrissa had liked. In Port Del Mar, her mother's shadow was overpowering. She had been guilty by association for most people. The rumor mill was going to have so much fun with this.

"Yes. They're mine. They're my *brothers*."

Confusion clouded his face. "I didn't know you had any brothers."

A very unladylike snort escaped her. "Join the club." She rubbed the bridge of her nose. All she wanted was to get to her father's house and hide under the quilt her great-grandmother had made for her sixteenth birthday. At least she hadn't taken that one with her to Missouri, or it would be gone too. She turned back to her newly found brother. "Bennett, what's going on?"

"Nothin'." He rolled his shoulder but couldn't dislodge Reno's hand. "This guy's just being a jerk. He needs to leave kids alone."

Reno gave her a slanted smile, obviously not offended by the comment. "I don't think the beef jerky and Dr Pepper accidentally fell into the pocket of his hoodie." He looked back at Bennett with one eyebrow raised.

She gasped. "You're stealing?"

The eight-year-old shrugged. "I was hungry. It's overpriced. You said you don't buy sodas."

She dropped down on her haunches and tried to look him in the eye. He had a talent for staring right over her shoulder as if she didn't exist. "If you were that hungry, you should have talked to me. Stealing is never okay. We're almost home and you can have a full meal."

His gaze cut to her. "Not my home." Hostility burned, covering up the hurt caused by their mother. "Mom said stores like this mark everything way up because they know half of it'll be taken. It didn't hurt anyone."

Ray-Ray eagerly nodded as he stepped in front of his big brother, his eyes wide. "She said that they didn't mind if kids took stuff, it was…" He looked up at his brother.

"Charity," Bennett offered. He shrugged. "They'll just right it off as a donation."

She closed her eyes and took a deep breath. The reality of her mother's problems had become clear to her long ago. Alcohol and drugs changed a person. It took control and had to be the center of attention. There's no telling what the boys had been exposed too. It shouldn't surprise her that she had taught her sons to steal as a way of life. The woman had stolen everything from her own daughter and from the church where Lyrissa had worked part-time.

It was less than twenty-four hours ago that the church had called to say that they had Dee, her mother, on video, walking out with all the petty cash that had been in Lyrissa's desk. Her mother had used her keys to steal from the church. Who did that?

Lyrissa had rushed home to find her apartment and checking account stripped clean. Only the boys were left behind.

She reached out to take Bennett's hand, but he pulled back. Ray-Ray pressed himself closer to his big brother, looking at her with fear in his eyes.

After only a few weeks of knowing each other, the boys were still reserved around her. Asking them to trust another adult was too much. All they knew was a mother who had walked out on them. They hadn't been blessed with someone like her father. A man whose compassion and unconditional love was an anchor in the worst storms.

He had always welcomed Dee back into their lives. No questions asked. Lyrissa had made a promise to herself to never be in that situation. Loving someone who only wanted a good time had to be fun at first, but it only led to heartbreak and misery. But the moment Dee knocked on her door with the boys, Lyrissa had welcomed them into her small apartment.

She was too much like her sweet father, foolishly optimistic. Where did that get her? Instead of reconnecting with the woman who never acted like a mother, she was now responsible for two young boys.

She was already messing it up.

And here stood Reno Espinoza, witnessing it all. This was why she never had gone into town the few times she had visited her dad and grandmother.

People knew her mother. It was so embarrassing, being the daughter of the town drunk. They looked at her father with a mix of pity and disgust. How could he love a woman like that? They had always eyed Lyrissa with suspicion.

All they saw was Dee.

Back in high school, after the pastor's gentle *intervention* that day, she knew she'd never be more than *Dee's daughter*, no matter how hard she worked to prove otherwise. She had begged her father to take her away. To start over somewhere fresh. But his mother-in-law needed him to run the ranch and Dee might come back. As much as she loved her father, she prayed to never be like him.

He had finally agreed to call his cousins and arranged for Lyrissa to finish her last year of high school in Dallas.

She hated and loved her father for his loyalty and capacity for forgiveness. But this was too much, even for the sweetest man she knew. Now, she was bringing home two boys who carried her father's name but weren't his blood. And they were caught stealing their first day in town.

She was in over her head.

Hand out in front of the boys, she stared Bennett in the eye. "Give me everything you put into your pockets. And listen to me. Our mother has an illness. You know stealing is wrong. Don't ever try to justify it again. You are my responsibility now and there will be no stealing, lying *or* cheating."

Heat spread up her neck and over her cheeks as she stood and looked at Reno. "Thank you for bringing him to me."

"You're heading to your dad's? He didn't say anything about—" he glanced at the boys "—you coming home. Does he know?"

Why did her family have to be such a mess? People in the store were starting to stare. Before the sun set, rumors would be everywhere. "I just called last night. We've been on the road all day. Thank you for bringing him to me and not..." She sighed. "Thanks. We need to be going."

Reno reached over and took the items Bennett had taken. After placing them in a red basket he carried, he looked back at her. "Let me get these as a welcome-back-to-town gift and to let you know all is forgiven for leaving me high and dry for homecoming." Giving her a charming smile, he winked.

Heat climbed up her neck. *Great, my whole face will be strawberry red soon.*

She took a few deep breaths, but she knew there was no stopping the scarlet splotches. "I…" Not knowing what to say, she bit her bottom lip. So, she hadn't sent a text.

It had been the Wednesday before the dance that the pastor had accused her of stealing. In her humiliation, she had figured Reno wouldn't want to be seen with her. Even though he had just been a sophomore and she'd been a senior, he had been a varsity player in their small school and was loved by everyone. It was clear she had been a pity date for him. Her best friend—who happened to be one of his sisters had probably made him. Now he caught her brothers stealing. *Please God, let the ground open beneath me.*

He leaned in closer to her, his forehead wrinkled in concern. "Sorry. If I had known that would make you uncomfortable, I wouldn't have said anything." Sincerity had replaced the teasing glint from earlier. "Did you know that Belle De La Rosa confessed and returned the money after she heard you had been blamed?"

Her mouth dropped open. "Belle?" That family might have had it worse than Lyrissa. At least she'd had her father and grandmother in her corner. Those kids had been all alone after the death of their mother. "I didn't know."

"She felt awful." He laid one large hand flat on his chest. "Really, no hard feelings." He gave her a genuine smile and squeezed her arm before dropping his hand. With a gentle nudge of his elbow, he winked again. The charmer was back. "Another underclassmen might have been scarred for life. Thankfully, my resilient personality protected the fragile teenage boy's ego from harm. My sisters all agreed it was good for me. Humbling."

He glanced at the boys, then grew serious. "Please, let me buy these for you to prove there are no ill feelings and send you out to your father with happy bellies. Your dad is one of my favorite people, you know." He guided them to the side doors to check out.

"Mine too." Her father deserved to be respected and she loved that Reno saw him for the kind human he was.

"What about the truck?" Ray-Ray asked.

She stopped. Dread knotted her stomach. "What truck?"

"Mama took mine, so Benny gave this one to me." He pulled a mini metal truck from the front pocket of his jacket and held it out to her.

"Ray-Ray," Bennett said between gritted teeth. "I gave that to you."

"But she said no more stealing." The sweet boy looked at his older brother in confusion.

Reno took the truck and tossed it in the basket. "Anything else, guys? Come clean now or suffer the consequences."

"What's that?" Ray-Ray looked between the two adults.

"It'll be up to your sister, but it usually involves chores no one wants to do. Mucking stalls, shoveling manure into a compost bin, and there is always the old pulling weeds from the pastures."

Bennett rolled his eyes and crossed his arms.

Ray-Ray shook his head. "That doesn't sound fun. What's manure?"

"Lyrissa? Lyrissa Martinez?" A woman with unnatural red hair touched her arm. "I thought that was you. Hi, Reno."

She hugged him, then turned to Lyrissa. A well-manicured hand rested on his arm as if staking a claim.

Madilyn House. Her throat went dry. The inadequacies she had grown up with surged into her system. *Maddy.* Why did she complain to God about seeing Reno? This was so much worse.

As nice as Reno had been, Maddy was the opposite. In school, the girl had taken every opportunity to put Lyrissa down. She was the one who had blamed her for the church's missing money.

She would never make the mistake of coming to town, ever again. Small town homecomings were not her thing. The past was better off forgotten.

* * *

Reno stiffened at Maddy's possessiveness. Ever since she'd returned to help her mom with the flower shop, she had made it clear she was interested in him. He had told her as gently as he could that it was a big no from him, but since he wasn't dating anyone else, she didn't think he really meant it.

Being nice was sometimes a huge pain. With a sigh, he shifted his attention to the two boys standing next to Lyrissa. He knelt to be eye level with them, then rested one arm across his knee. The move also dislodged Maddy's hold on him. *Two birds. One stone.*

She was being nosy, and he didn't want to give her any more information about Lyrissa and her brothers. He nodded. "As a welcome-to-town, I'm going to get these for you. Why don't you also go ahead and pick up your favorite chips."

Ray-Ray glanced at Lyrissa, then gave him a shy grin before turning to pick out a bag. Bennett shrugged as if showing any gratitude would make him weak. Lyrissa had her work cut out for her with that one.

"Which ones are plain? I like plain." The little boy looked up at Reno.

A moment of panic blurred his vision. He had not been prepared to read. All the bags had the same design. He blinked then forced a laugh and rubbed the boy's shoulders. "It's the start of a new adventure. Be brave and grab one. Then guess what flavor it is."

Ray-Ray grinned and nodded. Muscles he didn't realize were tensed relaxed. He had been caught off guard. He had spent his life pretending he could read, and no one had caught on yet. Surprise attacks were the worst. Making sense of all the lines and shapes seemed so easy for everyone else.

Needing to get away from the situation, he stood and grabbed a couple cups of fruit. "It was good seeing you, Maddy. They're running late. They need to beat that storm rolling in." He placed his hand on the back of the smallest one's shoulder and moved them away from the town gossip and toward the register at the other end of the store.

The woman didn't take the hint. She stood in front of Lyrissa, not letting her pass. With a big friendly smile that didn't hide the excited glint in her eyes, she forced Lyrissa to interact with her.

Maddy wanted to be the first to get a juicy story, so she'd have something exciting to talk about. It didn't matter if it was all true or not or if it hurt someone. "So, it's not Martinez anymore? I hadn't heard you got married."

Her smile tight, Lyrissa shook her head. "I didn't."

Maddy looked between the boys and Lyrissa. "Your dad didn't say anything about being a grandfather. That's so weird. When my oldest brother had his first, everyone in town knew about it." She chuckled. "They were so excited about being grandparents."

Stepping around her, Lyrissa held her forced smile. "They're my brothers."

Mouth opened, Maddy was wordless for a moment. "Oh. Well, that would explain why your father isn't bragging. I just…" She waved her hand as if to gather the right words, and the spark in her gaze burned brighter.

Reno needed to intercede before this meeting spiraled into even murkier waters.

"Maddy." He gently took the hand of the younger brother and moved around her. "Lyrissa and the boys have been in the car for hours and want to get to the ranch. You can talk later." He glanced at Lyrissa. Her smile was softer as she nodded to him and walked around Maddy. How had he forgotten how stunning she was? She wasn't the stereotypical beauty. *Pretty* was too tame a word.

Her thick curls were dark with streaks of fierce red that the scrunchie couldn't contain. But it was her eyes that made his breath seize in his chest. They were a bold green with shattered flakes of gold surrounded by thick black lashes.

To an outsider, she had the look of a fiery warrior, no matter how much she wanted to blend into the background and disappear.

Back in school, she had been at war with her looks. His sister had said no one really knew the real Lyrissa. She had always intrigued him. Over the years, that type of curiosity usually got him in trouble.

"Y'all want to get out to the ranch, right?" He gave everyone his best smile and guided the boys around Maddy. As they made their way to the cashier, Reno tossed a few of the BBQ sandwiches in the basket. "You can't come to Bucee's and not get the chopped."

Lyrissa stiffened. "Really, Reno. This is too much."

Her skin was pale. It looked as if she might be sick. He sat the basket on an available counter. As the girl started ringing up the items, Lyrissa fumbled through her purse.

He rested his hands on hers. "Let me do this. And don't worry about Maddy. She just returned home after a divorce and is not in a good place."

She glanced over her shoulder, then at the boys. They were hanging back.

The youngest blinked at them as if he weren't sure they wouldn't leave him here. Reno's sister Savannah and Lyrissa had been good friends. He knew too many of the details of how hard Dee

Martinez had made her daughter's life. This new situation with the boys and her mother must have rubbed her nerves raw. And now she was back in the town she wanted to escape.

She leaned in close, keeping her head down. "What kind of lesson will this teach the boys if I let you—"

Reno shook his head at her. "Don't. I remember being hungry all the time at that age. When I lost my dad, it helped when others saw me. They've lost their mom."

"Your father died. Their...our mother made horrible, selfish choices."

"Yeah. But losing a parent shakes up your world, no matter how or why they left. Let me do this. It makes me happy and lately I haven't had a lot to be happy about." *Ugh. Too much personal information.* Now why did he go and say that?

And in a second, the self-pity in her eyes turned to concern. "What happened?"

Great. He had wanted her to stop feeling guilty and now she was worried about him. He wasn't sure if this was better or worse.

He put his smile back on. Complaining was something he never did. His family had already been through too much because of him.

She shook her head. "Sorry. It's none of my business."

"It's okay. No big secret." He shrugged then added a handful of candy bars to the growing pile of food. He could share the parts of his life everyone knew already. The real secrets he had kept to himself had been buried far too long to say them aloud now.

"I'm just wallowing in a little self-pity. My sister and I started a construction business, and it was going great, but she fell in love and they moved away. I mean, I'm happy for Savannah getting her happy-ever-after, but I'm feeling a little left behind. She considered you a good friend. So, helping you helps me feel better. See, totally selfish." He made sure to give her the grin that his sisters said gave him his irresistible dimples.

"Sorry. I haven't spoken to Savannah for over a year. Where is she?"

Not wanting to get into it, he shrugged and gathered the bags. "Come on. Let's get y'all to the ranch." He could get her and the boys to the safety of the ranch. That was the least he could do for her. He smiled.

No one needed his bad mood to make things worse.

Chapter Two

Lyrissa's stomach was in knots. She just wanted to get out of town and hide on the ranch. As they walked toward the first set of sliding doors, they opened.

Reno followed them. She stopped next to the red carts and shopping baskets. The camping chairs and fire pits lining the glass wall caught the boys' attention. Thunder rumbled through the air. The clouds billowed as they threatened the earth with a heavy downpour.

A few people hurried by, going into the store. One of them called out a greeting to Reno.

Lightning flashed and a strong wind warned them to move to shelter.

Her skin felt too tight for her body as she scanned the parking lot. "It's probably better for you if you're not seen with us." She glanced at the boys. "You know Maddy is going to start some wild rumor. I really appreciate your help. Thank you."

She took her youngest brother's small hand and went out the sliding glass doors.

The sky opened and heavy raindrops fell hard. Lyrissa fumbled for a small umbrella in her backpack and when she opened it, the wind flipped it inside out. She adjusted it and used the wind to pop it back in place. "Come on." She would not cry. "We can make a run for it."

The small boy shook his head and looked down where the water was gathering. "My socks'll get wet. I hate wet socks."

Reno and she looked down at his feet at the same time. Heavy tape barely held together his sneakers. Should she go back inside and buy him a new pair? Before she could make a decision, Reno picked him up and carried him like a football. Pulling his Carhartt jacket over to shield them from the rain. He nodded to Lyrissa to lead the way.

"Really, you've already helped too—"

"Nope. The longer we stand here, the wetter everyone gets. Where are you parked?" He shifted Ray-Ray and the boy giggled.

With a reluctant nod, she put an arm around Bennett to pull him under the umbrella then jogged to her car. Each step slashed the quickly rising water.

She used the key fob to unlock the doors and handed the umbrella to Bennett. Reno slid Ray-

Ray into the back seat. Water dripped from his hair and into his eyes.

She pulled her wallet out and took out a ten. She hated being a charity case. "Let me pay at least part of—"

"Nope."

The strap of her purse slipped, and she adjusted it. She wrapped her thin jacket closer. "Thank you." She nodded to the boys, hoping they understood.

"Thank you for keeping my feet out of the water." Ray-Ray's tentative grin melted her heart.

"You're very welcome. Once you get settled into the ranch, we'll have to get you some boots."

Ray-Ray smiled bigger. Stepping back, Reno closed the door and jogged back to the storefront. Reno had always made everyone around him smile. It was a gift he had. She pushed the wet strands of hair off her face and glanced at the rearview mirror. "Ready to go home?"

Bennett crossed his arms and glared at the truck parked next to them. Ray-Ray nodded. "I like Texas."

"You're going to love the ranch." She hoped she was right. Her father had told her God had a plan and it would all work out. She hoped it was true, but she had seen it go wrong so many times before that it was hard for her to have her father's kind of faith. Maybe one day she would.

* * *

Reno watched as Lyrissa and her two brothers pulled out of the parking lot. He wasn't sure why seeing her had hit him so hard. Yeah, she had stood him up, but he hadn't mooned over her or anything. Life happened and they moved on.

So why did seeing her stir up his insides in a weird way? With a deep sigh, he shrugged it off and turned back into the store to get his coffee. With the boys and Lyrissa's return, he'd gotten distracted and forgot his whole reason for stopping.

He shook his head, trying to get the extra water off. This would have been a good day to wear his hat. After wiping his boots on the oversize welcome mat, he went back into the store.

It didn't take long for Maddy to reappear. "I noticed the age of that oldest boy. The math is not hard to do. Is he yours? Did you know about him?"

He dropped his head and stifled a groan. He poured a packet of sugar into his coffee, then a touch of cream, and stirred the hot liquid. Maddy was a gossip.

In school, she had been the kind to stir up drama then sit back and watch the fireworks like it was a personal performance for her entertainment. Avoiding her had always been his plan of action. He had never understood people who were entertained by others' suffering. She stood next to him, sipping her coffee like she had all day to wait him out.

He and Lyrissa hadn't had that type of relationship, but it wasn't any of Maddy's business. "They're her brothers. Have a good day. I need to get to work." With the rain, he wouldn't be going out to the jobsite, but she didn't need to know that. He walked past her.

She followed. Of course she did. She had an agenda.

"Y'all were dating when she took off all of a sudden. It was the middle of her senior year and *poof* she just left. We were just sophomores. So, was she pregnant? That's why she left, isn't it? It makes sense."

Maybe to get away from gossips? "Nope. She went to stay with her cousins in Dallas." Why was he even engaging in this conversation? He pulled his wallet out of his back pocket then nodded to Maddy's coffee and fresh fruit cup.

"Oh, you didn't have to do that. Thank you." She followed him through the sliding glass doors. "So, she stayed in touch with you. Did you know she had a baby? Is he yours?"

"Those are her brothers." But the facts weren't important to Maddy if she thought she had a good story.

"No. I don't think so. We would have heard if

her mother had more kids. Those boys are hers. Why is she lying? That Wimberly girl came back into town with Adrian's kid. That blew everyone out of the water. He was going to be sheriff and now they live in Canada."

She put her hand on his shoulder. "Reno, you're a nice guy. Be careful. She could totally be here to ruin your life. It would be just like her. That kid kind of looks like you."

"Maddy, stop. Those two boys are her mother's sons. They have enough to deal with. Leave it alone. She left because someone lied to the pastor and told him she had stolen money from the church."

Eyes wide, she stepped back as if he had yelled or lifted his fist at her. "I did see her with the offerings. I just reported what I saw. Don't be mad at me. I'm on your side. She's always been trouble. Be careful."

"Bye, Maddy." He was profoundly grateful that his work truck was on the opposite side of the monster parking lot.

The rain had pulled back into a drizzle as he made his way along the sidewalk. He should have said more, but no matter what he said, Maddy was going to start a line of rumors that had no truth.

Without a conscious thought, he looked to the spot where Lyrissa's Mazda had been parked.

There was something on the ground. He narrowed his gaze. It was a wallet. He stepped closer. It was the one she had pulled out when she had tried to give him money. It was drenched in rainwater.

He picked up the worn leather wallet and flipped open the silver latch. It was well made but well used too. The insides were still mostly dry. On the top was her driver's license. He closed it then tucked it inside the pocket of his jacket. Her father was on his list of people to check on later this week.

Mundo Martinez just got moved up. He couldn't believe the youngest was named after Raymundo. Dee hadn't been home in over ten years, so the boy wasn't his.

And now Lyrissa was bringing Dee's sons to the ranch and Mundo was okay with this?

He didn't know many men who would take in their ex-wife's children from other relationships. Mundo was one of a kind and the nicest man he had ever met. The problem with being nice? People take advantage.

Was Lyrissa going to drop the boys and run back to her life in Missouri or was she at least going to stick around long enough to make sure the boys were settled?

He should call his mom. She was great at helping people who were in over their heads. Not that Lyrissa gave any indication that she wanted help. The times she had visited the ranch in recent years, she never came to town. It was a clear message that she wanted nothing to do with the people of Port Del Mar.

The wallet would be easy to slip into the mailbox at the end of the road. A text to Mundo would ensure she got it. There was no need to hand-deliver it to her.

Not one single reason.

Chapter Three

"Stop making that weird noise," Bennett snapped at his brother.

"I'm not making a weird noise." Ray-Ray opened his mouth wider and made another nonsensical sound. "*Mmmmmoowt*. Stop looking at me."

"You're such a baby. You wouldn't know I was looking at you if you weren't looking at me."

Ray-Ray yelled and swung to hit Bennett.

"Boys. Stop." The pounding of the rain echoed the pounding behind her eyes. But she took a breath as they fell silent. She was in over her head. She had been an only child and had no clue how siblings interacted. The Espinoza family was the only one she had ever been around, and they certainly didn't act like this.

Was this normal for brothers or had their mother left deep psychological scars? That was a ridiculous question. How could they not be scarred? Tomorrow, she would investigate therapy.

She snorted. They all needed some good counseling. There was no way the path of destruction left by her mother didn't affect them all. Her father claimed that God had him and his faith was all he needed, but really?

Then again, there had to be something to it. When she had called him not knowing what to do, he immediately and without hesitation told her to bring them to the ranch. These were his ex-wife's children from other men, and he told her to bring them home. That was a man speaking from a heart of gold.

Everyone in town was going to see him as a fool. Maddy crossed her mind. Or they'll say she's a liar, and that the boys are really Lyrissa's own.

People annoyed her. Her father was too kind. Too forgiving. The world chewed up and spit out people like him. Her mother definitely did.

And here she was, bringing more of her mother's drama to her father's doorstep. She should take the boys to her grandmother's house. They might not be related to her father, but they were her grandmother's grandsons. Mew-Maw had always worried about not having anyone to continue the family ranch.

Maybe the boys were God's gift to her grandmother.

She glanced at the dashboard clock. Her brain was in a fog. Going without sleep for this long was not conducive to clear thinking. Home was so close.

Once on the ranch, they would come up with a plan together. Hopefully, it wouldn't include coming back to town, ever.

She turned right into the entry. The once-white fence leaned as if too tired to stand. One strong wind would take it down. The main post for the front gate wasn't in any better shape. Why hadn't her father told her he needed help? Of course, she hadn't asked.

Her dad's house, the old foreman's place, came into view. It was closest to the front gate. The main house where her grandmother lived was a little farther down. The biggest barns were in between the two. She had spent her childhood wearing out a path between the houses and barns. It was the best part of her childhood.

This was exactly the stability the boys needed after the chaos wrought by their mother. Hoping they would love it as much as she had, she glanced in the rearview mirror. Ray-Ray's face was pressed against the glass.

"Look, Benny. Cows. Oh, and there's someone riding a horse." Benny didn't seem impressed by Ray-Ray's excitement.

The rain had stopped. "That's your grandmother." It was hard to see it was a woman well into her sixth decade, with the long yellow rain slicker, but her grandmother loved riding out in all sorts of weather. When her father worried, Mew-Maw would laugh and say the more challenging, the more alive she felt. Just because she was closing in on seventy didn't mean she had to stop living.

Lyrissa dodged the biggest potholes, but it was impossible to miss them all. Her little car would be covered in mud. Not getting stuck would be a blessing. "She likes to ride one of the horses to check the mail," she told the boys.

That had them quiet as they stared at the horse and rider. That was encouraging, so she went on. "Your grandmother is excited to meet you. I call her Mew-Maw. We'll visit with my dad, but I think we'll be living with her."

"She's not our real grandmother." Bennett crossed his arms and swung his gaze away from the window.

"She's our mother's mother. That makes her your grandmother."

He frowned. "But I thought we were visiting your father's ranch."

"Our family is complicated. It's our grandmother's ranch. It's been in the Herff family for seven generations. We make nine. My father lives here to help her. He loves his mother-in-law and working on the land. Our mother wanted to live in the city."

"Apparently in all of them." Bennett's sarcastic words were too bitter and cynical for his years.

"Where she goes doesn't matter anymore. This is your home now. It's a forever home and no one is going to take it from you. I'm so glad you're here now. They are too. There're only a few days of school left, so we'll get you registered for next year."

"School?" Ray-Ray perked up. "I want to go. I'm old enough?"

Bennett scoffed. "School's stupid."

The road ahead of them would be rougher than the road under them now. The three-bedroom, one-bath house she grew up in came into view. The roofline over the old porch sagged in a sad smile. But the man standing on the top step wore a huge grin. He waved and came toward them carrying a huge umbrella like a walking cane. Her father, Raymundo "Mundo" Martinez, acted as if he had been waiting for this day his whole life.

As he came down the steps, thunder rumbled and rain started to fall in huge, heavy drops again.

Her heart tugged at the sight of her daddy waiting for them. She pulled up to the side of the house, then cut the engine and turned to face the boys behind her. "My dad is the sweetest, kindest human you will ever meet. Please treat him with respect."

Before either boy could reply, her father had the back door opened, angling the colorful umbrella to block the rain. "Hey sweetheart! So sorry about the rain, but I'm happy you're home. Look at these two fine young men. Welcome. I'm excited to show you the place. This is your home too, you know. Have you ever been on a ranch?" He helped Ray-Ray out of his seat belt.

"No, sir," the shy boy said with a small grin. "Do I need boots and a hat? I don't have 'em."

Bennett snorted. "We're not staying. Our mom will come and get us." He hadn't moved to get out.

Her dad nodded. "This is a good place to wait for her. I'm glad you're here. She grew up on this land and knows it well. In the meantime, we can get to know each other. Love my daughter to pieces but always wanted a couple of boys too." His smile went even wider. "This will be great, you'll see. God has a plan and purpose for each of us. Let's get you out of the rain. I'll show you to your room."

Did God have a plan? She sighed. Now was not the time to question her father's faith. "Dad. I think it's best if we move in with Mew-Maw. The house is bigger and—"

"Stop right there. You said you were coming home. This house might be smaller, but it's a good home. You and the boys will be staying here. Your room is here, and they can have the loft. It's been waiting for them before I knew they were here. God knew." His eyes shined with emotion. Lips pressed tightly together, he smiled and nodded. "The three of you belong here."

With a heavy sigh, she pulled herself out of the car, and went around to open the trunk. Her father was nice but also one of the most quietly stubborn people she knew, only after her grandmother.

"Looks like we'll be staying here, boys." There was no way she could tell her father no. Not after that speech.

He took them to the porch at a run. She grabbed the few bags they had and followed. Her father believed what he just said—she knew he did—but she was having a hard time coming to grips with God's plan for her.

Earlier this week, she was on track and had a clear purpose. Now her life was being derailed by their train wreck of a mother. If God was in control, then how did this happen to her and the boys?

On the porch, she stopped and looked back over the front pastures. A warm hand gripped her shoulder. "Sweetheart. It's all going to be okay. I'm thrilled you're home. Right now, you don't see it, but I promise God has the perfect path that is just for you if you stay faithful and open to his will."

"I was on a great path, Daddy. Until she flew in and destroyed it. But this time it's not just me." She looked at the two innocent boys left behind and couldn't hold the question back. "How can this be God's will?"

He pulled her into his arms and pressed his forehead to hers. "Right now, everything looks ugly and you're hurting. Your mother has been lost for a while now. That's the danger of free will. My heart aches that you've been hurt by her again. But we'll get through this, and you'll be stronger on the other side."

With a sigh, she kissed his cheek. He stepped back and took the two worn duffel bags from her. He turned to the boys and smiled. "Come on, boys. I'll show you to your room."

He was opening the door when they heard a truck approach the house. "Is it Mom?" The hope in Bennett's voice broke her heart. They all turned.

"Nope, not yet. It's a good friend of mine. You know him, Lyrissa. It's Reno Espinoza. I wasn't expecting him till later this week."

The well-worn work truck stopped behind her car and Reno jumped out.

"It's the man from the store. The one who

caught us stealing." Ray-Ray sounded too happy for that statement. She groaned.

"Stealing?" Her father frowned.

"Hi again, Reno," she yelled in hopes of distracting her father.

"Hey!" Reno jogged to the porch as he pulled something out of his jacket. "Mundo, *como esta*?"

"*Bien*, I'm good. Thank God for the beautiful rain and bringing these fine boys to the ranch."

"We had the pleasure to meet in town. I told 'em they'd be needing some boots and a good hat." He ran his hands though his wet hair and pushed it back. "I could have used mine today." He laughed. The kind of laugh that spread joy and made everyone within hearing distance join him. Golden-brown eyes sparkled. Someone this happy all the time didn't take life seriously, Lyrissa thought.

"This was dropped in the parking lot. Thought you might get worried when you found it gone." His eyebrows wiggled a couple of times. "Or you left it behind so I would follow you." With a wink, he reached toward her. She stepped back. It was dangerous to be too close to him. The proverbial flame that drew in the moths seeking warmth and light.

It was her wallet. He was trying to give it back to her. His hands were large and strong, the fingers graceful despite—or maybe because of—

the dark golden brown of his work-worn skin. They looked warm to the touch. As warm as his golden-brown eyes and smile. She jerked her head to the side to look away from him.

She looked in her purse as if she needed to check if hers was missing. Obviously, it was. With a deep breath, she took it from him as if they were handling explosives.

Warm fingers brushed hers. She cleared her throat. "I didn't even realize it was missing. Thank you." She made the mistake of studying his face and their eyes locked. The Espinozas were a beautiful family and Reno was...

"What's this about you catching the boys stealing?" Her father's voice broke her train of thought and the staring contest.

Shaking her head, she took a moment to center herself. She was tired. Any feelings or attraction she had for Reno was just her brain not functioning at full capacity.

She needed to get the boys settled and a good sleep. All this messing about would clear out and she'd be fine. For now, she would just keep her distance. Tucking her wallet in her purse, she stepped as far away from his warmth as she could.

He would be leaving in the next few minutes.

Reno watched as she pulled away from him. Apparently, as far as she could get. Had he done something to upset her? He shook his head and turned to Mundo. "There had been a misunderstanding. But we straightened it out. Lyrissa did promise the boys that there would be a full meal here."

Lightning streaked through the sky and thunder shook the foundation of the house. "Yes. Yes. Let's get y'all inside." Her father waved his hand to the door.

She quickly turned away from him and reached for the door.

"Reno, join us." Mundo clapped a hand on his back.

Lyrissa froze and glanced at him in a panic. So, she didn't want him to stay. "Thank you, sir. But I need to—"

"I won't hear any excuses. With this weather you won't be working on the Carter's barn. You might as well come in and get something to eat."

"Is that our grandmother? Is she a real cowboy?" Ray-Ray yelled from the railing, barely out of the rain. He pointed down the long drive. The lone figure covered head to boot in a yellow rain slicker was running a horse full-out toward the house.

With a big grin, Mundo joined the boy. "That there is your grandmother. Lyrissa calls her Mew-Maw. Stubborn woman. I told her I would get the mail. She's the most real cowboy you'll ever meet."

The gray horse came to a sliding stop at the base of the steps. The tall figure swung a leg over and dismounted. She moved up the steps and the horse followed. Lyrissa's dad pulled Ray-Ray back.

Throwing the reins over the porch railing, Edith Herff, the sixty-eight-year-old matriarch, dropped the hood of her rain slicker. She turned and stared at them, hand on her hips. "This rain can't seem to make up its mind if it's coming or going. The forecast said slight chance of drizzle. Being a weatherman must be the easiest paycheck ever. If I was wrong that many times, we wouldn't have a ranch at all."

She pulled off her cowboy hat and shook the rain off. Her silver hair was pulled back into a thick braid. "These must be my new grandsons. They look strong." She grinned. "It's been some time since we had any male children in the family. Shame you've been gone so long. But you're here now, that's all that matters. That youngest is the spitin' image of my daddy. I'll have to show you the pictures."

"Hey, Mew-Maw." Lyrissa stepped forward. The boys looked as if an alien had just popped out of a flying saucer. "This is Bennett and Raymundo. He goes by Ray-Ray."

"The little one's named after you?" She squinted at her son-in-law.

"Appears so."

"Well, that girl of mine is something else." She shoved her hat back on. "Hello, Reno. Don't think there'll be much outside work done today." She eyed Lyrissa then winked. "Are there other things that you're interested in? Maybe something new that just showed up on the ranch?"

"Mew-Maw! I dropped my wallet in the Buc-ee's parking lot and he was kind enough to bring it out so I wouldn't worry." Her gaze darted across the pastures, looking everywhere but at him.

"Aww. Such a good boy. Your momma raised you right." She patted Reno on the arm.

"There's a horse on the porch?" Bennett looked at them as if they were from another world and he didn't understand the language.

"Well, where else should I put him? The barn's way over there and I don't want him standing in the rain."

"Can I touch him?" Ray-Ray asked.

"Sure. Come here. I need to get the mail out of the bag anyway."

The boys tentatively followed her to the far end of the long porch, staring in awe at the big gelding.

Her father opened the door. "I have *papas*

and huevos rancheros on the stove, ready to be eaten. Ya'll come in when you're finished with the horse."

"What's that?" Ray-Ray asked.

"Some really good stuff and the real reason I braved the storm to come over." Reno rubbed his stomach. "Mundo's potatoes and eggs wrapped up in a tortilla is the best. Well, second best. No one compares to my mom's."

Her father laughed as they entered the house. "That's the absolute truth."

The cabin was modest. The front living area had a sofa and two rocking chairs with stuffed seating. A large fireplace filled one wall. There was a TV in the corner, but other than the evening news, Reno had never seen it on.

A hallway led to two bedrooms with a bathroom in between them. "Your room is ready for you," he told Lyrissa as he went down the two steps into the dining room and kitchen area.

To the left was a spiral staircase that led to a large loft and an unfinished bathroom. It had been like that for years. When Reno had asked if he wanted to finish it out, Mundo had said there was no reason. Years ago, Mundo had dreamed of his wife coming home and a couple more children. Reno couldn't imagine how this must feel for the man.

Lyrissa glanced at him then. He should leave.

He didn't belong here. The last thing he wanted was to make her uncomfortable in this very private family reunion.

Before he could make an escape, though, Edith came in behind him with the boys and they blocked his exit. He was trapped.

Lyrissa needed to get over herself. There was absolutely no reason for her to be acting this way around Reno. He was her father's friend.

Mundo moved to the cabinet and pulled down paper plates. "Reno, don't think about leaving. We need to talk about that bathroom upstairs. I finally have a reason to make it a working restroom. These two will need it as soon as possible. I knew God had more children for me to raise, but I didn't see how it would happen." He shook his head. "I shouldn't have doubted." Her heart squeezed at her dad's joy over this unexpected curveball in his life.

"Lyrissa, why don't you take the boys up and show 'em their room. There is a double bed on one side and a set of bunk beds on the other, so they can pick which one they want. Reno, can you take a look?"

Still standing at the entrance of the kitchen, the man looked like he was planning an escape.

"Please stay, Reno." Mundo asked in a soft voice.

Ray-Ray was already halfway up the stairs when he stopped and looked up in awe. "Really? We get a room just for us?" He turned to her dad.

Lips tight, her father nodded. He blinked then smiled. "Especially for you. It's been waiting."

He bound up the last steps to the top then stopped and gasped. "Benny, it's huge. We each get a real bed. All our own." The unbelieving tone in his voice broke her heart. Where had they been staying?

Bennett had one hand on the railing but just stood there. Reno came up behind him. "Come on. Your brother's going to get first pick if you don't hurry."

With an obvious swallow, he nodded and moved up the staircase.

Reno followed with Lyrissa close behind. Ray-Ray was on the top bunk, bouncing. "Benny, this is fun."

"You shouldn't pick that one." Bennett sounded older than his years. "You could fall."

The little one scrambled down. "I'm careful. We could make the bottom one into a fort. That would be cool. We can hide in there."

As Ray-Ray climbed over all the beds, Reno went into the small bathroom that divided the loft into two spaces. "Your dad asked if I could finish it out." He turned around and leaned on the doorframe. "It has most of what's needed.

There are a few items to be bought. A little fram-
ing and detailing. The last thing will be connect-
ing to water. I've worked with a guy in town
who can do the plumbing. He's good and fair."

Ray-Ray bounced off the bed and ran to Reno,
then poked his head into the bathroom.

"We get our own bathroom too? I don't want to
ever leave." He darted to the other door behind the
bathroom and opened it up. "A closet! It's like a
secret room. This is the most greatest place ever."

"Don't get used to it. We won't be staying."
Bennett got up from the double bed and stood
by the railing, looking down into the kitchen. He
pulled the hood of his sweatshirt up and crossed
his arms.

"But they said it's our home," Ray-Ray said.

"Yeah. We've heard that before and it never
happened. People lie."

"Bennett." She wanted to put her arms around
him and pull him close. But he wouldn't welcome her comfort. She stood next to him and
mirrored his stance at the railing. They both
watched her father fixing their plates and setting the table. He was whistling.

"I know you've no reason to trust me or my
father. But this is your home. No matter what
happens. You are Herffs and there is nothing
you can do to change that. You're stuck with us."

He shrugged and she knew it was going to

take so much more than a few words to make him feel safe.

Reno came over and patted the sullen boy on the shoulder. "Come on down. You can ponder life and mope later. The food is on the table."

It didn't take long for everyone to settle around the old farm table. The wood was worn from decades of meals being served. Her father had them join hands for a prayer. The boys wiggled a bit but kept their heads bowed. With an *amen* he passed the tortilla basket around. Mew-Maw took a few bites while she flipped through the mail to separate the envelopes. Then she froze. Her green eyes came up and she made eye contact with Lyrissa, then her son-in-law.

She cleared her throat. "There's a letter from Dee." She held it out to her father. Everyone went quiet. Eating had stopped.

His hand shook as he took the envelope. As if expecting a bomb, he carefully opened it. After a reassuring smile to the boys, he looked down and silently read the letter. It was one page.

Lyrissa's stomach twisted. What new ways could her mother hurt the man who loved her so much?

He looked at the boys then at her. Moisture pooled on the bottom lid of his midnight eyes. He shook his head as if denying something. Everything in her readied for the worst.

Standing quickly, he knocked his chair back. It crashed to the ground, and he didn't seem to notice. The letter was crumpled in his fist.

She reached out for him with one hand and covered her heart with the other. What in the world had the letter said to get this reaction from her father? Something was wrong. In everything they had been through, her father had never cried. Never had an angry reaction. Whatever was in that letter had brought tears to his eyes.

"Daddy?"

Next to her, Reno stood. "Mundo, is there anything you need me to do?"

The urge to take his hand overwhelmed her. She couldn't reach her father. As if reading her mind, he wrapped his warm fingers around hers and gently squeezed. It shouldn't have comforted her, but it did.

"No. No" Her father looked at Bennett and made a muffled cry. He cleared his throat and stepped back. "I need a moment. Sorry." He rushed to the back door and into the storm.

Chapter Four

Stunned, Lyrissa looked at the fallen chair. Its carved legs pointing at her. The slam of the door echoed in her head. Not once in her whole life had she seen her father that upset.

She moved her gaze to her grandmother, then blinked, not sure what to do. The other woman jutted her chin to the door. "Me and the boys will finish up our meal then go out front to check on the horse."

The boys. All day she had reassured them how nice her father was. They looked at her but didn't seem too fazed by the outburst. Of course, growing up with Dee's drama, this was commonplace. "I'm going to check on Dad. Y'all enjoy your food."

Reno righted the chair. She walked out the back and scanned the area for her father. Dee wasn't even here, but still managed to ruin her father's happiness.

The screen door squeaked behind her. It was

Reno. With an easy and relaxed posture, he joined her. Hands in his pockets, he stared at the sky.

"Never seen Mundo react to anything like that before." His expression was gentle. "Do you mind if I check on him with you?"

Her immediate response was yes, she minded. This was a private matter. But the genuine concern in his face stopped her. Reno had been here for her father more than she had over the last few years.

With a quick jerk of her head, she kept walking to the barn. The rain had stopped. The smell of parched soil given a long drink floated around her. Fresh air filled her lungs. She wanted to stay and linger here.

Rainy days had always been her favorite on the ranch. But she didn't have the time. Nope, her mother had crushed the pleasant day from miles away.

"Any idea what the letter said?" Reno asked.

"With my mom, there's no telling. He's usually happy to get any word from her, so I don't know what could have caused this kind of reaction."

She glanced behind her to the house. "Maybe it's something to do with the boys. But when I called and told him about them, he was surprised but immediately told me to bring them home. He handled it with his usual calm attitude. What could be worse than learning about them?"

"He doesn't get ruffled easily and I've never seen him overreact. When he's upset, he goes there." Reno pointed to the stables. The large door was open, and lights were on.

The stables full of horses, hay and leather had been her sanctuary growing up. It had been a place to go when being in the world had hurt too much.

The tall man beside her stopped. "You know what. You're here. You should go. I'm not any good with…" He waved his hand in front of his chest as if stirring a pot.

"Feelings?"

He shrugged. "Emotional stuff. I'm good when someone needs a laugh or to forget their troubles. But your father seems really upset. I just wanted to make sure he was okay. You should go on without me."

Reno turned away from her.

Her stomach knotted. Fear of whatever was in the letter made her nauseous. "No. Don't go. I can't imagine what she told him. I haven't been around much. He might talk to you about the news she gave him. I don't know what he needs."

"Okay." With a sigh, Reno turned back and reached the large double door before she did. He

slid it a little farther open, then held it for her
while she walked into the old, familiar space.

"Dad?"

Rustling came from the tack room on the right
side of the corridor. He stepped out with a caddy
of grooming supplies in one hand and cubes of
alfalfa in the other.

With an uncharacteristic grunt, he shook his
head. "Go. Don't think I can talk about it right
now." He turned his back to them and headed
to the back stalls.

His jaw was rigid, there was so much pain and
anger in his eyes. She went to him and put her
hand on his arm, stopping him.

He looked away. "Are the boys okay?" he
asked. "I didn't mean to scare them."

"They're fine. Mew-Maw has them." She
moved in front of him, trying to make eye contact. "Daddy, what did that letter say?"

His tongue went over his bottom lip, then he
pressed his mouth into a hard straight line. Moving to the left, he broke contact with her and
went to the blue roan mare tied at the double
post in the open grooming area.

The only sounds were Reno's boots on the
century-old brick and the shifting of the stalled
horses. Reno came up behind her, placed his
hand on her shoulder. His presence created a
conflict inside her. There was a tension she

didn't like but also a calming reassurance that her father trusted him. Then again, her father loved her mother to a fault.

"Mundo, is there anything we can do?" he asked in a voice much calmer than anything she could manage. "I've never seen you this upset."

Putting the caddy down, her father remained silent. He shook his head. Then he went to the head of the horse and talked to her as he ran his hand under her jaw and down her neck.

She stood by helplessly as she watched the hands that raised her with love and gentleness shake. He moved from the front of the horse to the mare's side. He brushed her from the top of her shoulder down to her hooves.

"Daddy, you're scaring me. I know Dee. If you're protecting me, don't. We talk about everything, right? Why aren't you talking to me now? I've never seen you this angry."

He stopped and braced an arm on the horse's back. "When you were ten and your mother took you without telling me, I was this angry. I tried everything, then the police finally called. I was livid but she cried and asked for forgiveness. She promised me she would never take you again. I believed her. Just when I start thinking she can't do anything else to hurt us, she goes and proves me wrong."

Lyrissa's heart dropped to her stomach. She

wanted to scream at the frustration of seeing him like this and not being able to make it better. "Daddy, please tell me what she's done this time."

He leaned into the mare, pressing his forehead against her. "She…she…" He stepped back and brushed the mare's hindquarters with quick, jerky movements.

The lack of information was strangling her. She moved forward, but Reno reached for her hand and held her back. He nodded his head, suggesting she give her father space.

Her father grabbed a hoof-pick and a hard brush from the caddy and moved to the horse's front. He lifted a leg and worked on the inside of the hoof.

After a moment, he started talking again. "I tried to intervene with you. I really did. Once the addiction took control, I knew her actions hurt you. I knew. I worked hard to stand between you and the addiction. I thought if I prayed hard enough and stood on truth, she would come back… I would have the woman I loved back. I loved her and I loved you. I didn't know how to balance that. You had to be protected so I let her go and hoped she would find her way back to us. I never wanted my children to suffer."

"I'm fine, Daddy. You were always making me feel safe and loved. I know you loved her.

You've always said grace costs us nothing to give. You made sure to teach me that forgiveness releases the bitterness from our hearts. I'm not sure I'm there but you're my hero, Daddy, and I want to be more like you."

"It's not me you should strive to be but our Savior." He shook his head, and it dropped in defeat. "What if the price of grace becomes too much and it costs the well-being of the innocents? You're not unaffected by your mother's choices. The boys…" A soft straggling sound cut off his words.

The heartbreak and doubt tore her heart apart. He had always been so steadfast in his faith.

Moving to his side, she put a hand on his sagging shoulder. "The boys were out of your control. You can't blame yourself for that. But we have them now. They're safe."

She wanted to cry at the pain she saw in her father. The suffering her mother's addiction had caused them all. Her lungs were tightening. "Daddy, what's in that letter that changed everything?"

"I should've done more, but I put it in God's hands. It was a cop-out and I'm just weak."

She looked at Reno. Maybe he knew what to do.

"Mundo." Reno's voice was thick, but he had a dazzling smile on his face. "You just need to get it off your chest." He pushed his still-damp hair back. "Hey. Do you know what a rabbit needs after getting caught in the rain? A *hare* dryer."

She turned and glared at him and mouthed *What?* He shrugged his shoulders as if he had no other options. She groaned.

It was a mistake including him in this, but then again, she should have learned by now that relying on other people was a waste of time.

Reno wanted to slam his head against the old brick wall. He never handled emotional situations well, but really? A pathetic dad joke? He sighed and tried to ignore Lyrissa's obvious and justified irritation.

He cleared his throat. "It might help if you share what's in the letter."

"I didn't read the whole letter. Stopped at the second line. It all went blurry. I can't even speak the words." He stepped back and pulled the crumpled ball of paper out of his pocket.

Jaw gritted, he handed it to Reno. No clue what to do, he instinctively took it from the older man. Mundo wanted him to read it. Swallowing, he tried to get enough oxygen in his lungs to speak.

Mundo kept his gaze on the horse. The man's only daughter looked at Reno, waiting for him to start speaking. He had already disappointed her once today.

As he slowly unfolded the wadded-up paper, his mind raced. He took more care to smooth it out. *Now what?*

The horses shuffled as if they were also getting restless waiting for him. Heat pushed against his skin.

"Read it, Reno," Mundo said. "Read it aloud so Lyrissa will know that she's been right to cut her mom off. She's been right every time she's told me to let her go and move on."

"I don't want to be right, Daddy." Her voice was small, as if she was eight years old all over again.

"I thought if I gave her enough grace, she would come back but…" He swallowed hard and turned to Reno, lifting his chin. "Go ahead. Read it, Reno."

Maybe this time if he tried hard enough and really focused he wouldn't let down one of his favorite people. This man didn't deserve this kind of pain.

Pulling the paper straight, he tried to flatten it. The lines and shapes of the letters floated. Reno was going to be sick. He closed his eyes and took a few breaths. But when he looked at the paper again it was still gibberish.

At this point, he usually made a joke and either faked his way through reading aloud or passed it off to someone else without anyone being the wiser that he couldn't read.

Reno squinted at the paper. "I...uhm...forgot my contacts today." He handed the letter to Lyrissa. "Sorry. Would you read it?"

A frown crested her forehead. "When did you start wearing glasses?"

His stomach churned. That was the problem with people knowing him his whole life. He hated lying and people didn't usually challenge him. He stood in silence until she finally took the letter. Her hands shook. He was a complete heel forcing her to read the letter from her mother.

As soon as she looked down, she read. "'My dearest Raymundo. I'm so sorry that I'm just now writing this to you. It's eight years too late. Bennett's birthday is September nineteenth. If you count back the months, you'll know he's... yours.'"

Lyrissa's voice cracked and she looked up at her father. Mundo had his hand on the horse's neck and face buried in her mane.

"Daddy?"

He nodded without looking up. "Go on. That's where I stopped."

"Okay." She took a deep breath. Reno moved closer to her. None of them had known about the boy who was Mundo's son and Lyrissa's brother. He wasn't sure how to help them with this revelation, so he stood next to her and put one hand on Mundo's back.

She continued reading, tears trailing her cheeks.

"'I know what I've done is wrong.'" A very sarcastic snort escaped Lyrissa before she went back to reading. "'But I have to take the time to find myself and make it right. Then I'll come back for the boys and fix everything. I thought having the boys would help me, but I know now they are better off with you. I know I said the same thing when I called you to come get me in California, but I wasn't ready. The thought of going back to the ranch made me feel trapped. When I realized I was pregnant, I thought maybe it was a chance for me to have a do-over, because I messed up so much with our daughter. She's one hundred percent you and I wanted this baby to be mine. So, I kept him and didn't tell you that we had another child. Benny is your son. Little Ray-Ray's father is history, and we're better off without him. I wanted to give him a good strong name. You're the best man I know so I named him after you.'"

A soft sob came from Mundo. The kind of noise someone makes when they are trying to hold everything inside and it's too much. Lyrissa heard it too. She stumbled over the next words.

Reno wanted to take the paper and rip it to shreds. But it wouldn't make this go away. All he could do was stand next to Mundo and put his arms around the man's shaking shoulders.

"Do you want me to read the rest?"

Her father nodded without raising his head.

"'Nick is different than all the other men. We have a plan to make everything right. We have a perfect business venture. I just needed the money to become a full partner with him. Please tell...'" She paused, then took a deep breath.

"'Please tell Lyrissa I will pay her back for everything with interest. I'll make a donation to the church. I figure a good church supports those in need. It's for a worthy cause. I...'"

Lyrissa closed her eyes and tilted her head back. "How can she justify stealing from the church using my key?" She looked back down.

Reno wanted to reach for her and offer to read the rest of the letter. He hated his brain sometimes. Why couldn't he just learn to read? "I'm so sorry—"

She held up her hand, her jaw set. "I've got this. There's not much more."

"'Please, tell the boys that I love them. Once the business is making a profit—and I know it will—I promise I'll come to the ranch. Hopefully next summer. It will be a really fun time, I promise. I love you and always will. Give Lyrissa my love, even though I'm sure she hates me. I'll fix this—I promise I will.'"

Mundo wiped his face. Reno stood back and gave him room to move to Lyrissa. Her mouth was open and her eyes wide. All the signs of being shell-shocked were on her face.

"Daddy, is it true? How can Bennett be yours? She hasn't been to the ranch since I was in the sixth grade. This doesn't make any sense."

Mundo put one arm around her and pulled her into his barreled chest. He laid his cheek on the side of her head and stroked her back.

"It was after you went to Dallas. She called me in mid-January. She was in a real bad place. She was living on the streets, trying to get to shelters but kept being kicked out because of the drinking. She said she was going to end everyone's misery and called me to say goodbye. I told her to hang on and I'd come get her. I was so afraid of what I would find. But she was in the shelter waiting for me. She was clean and wanted to put the past behind her. She said the hope I gave her saved her life."

"Oh, Daddy. You never said anything."

"I didn't even tell your grandmother. I didn't want to worry y'all. It was winter so we had some downtime. I just said I needed to take care of some business. I thought that might be the time to bring her home. You know, hitting rock bottom and all that." He hugged his daughter tighter.

"But she didn't come home with you."

"She wanted to get her life in order before facing her mom. You know they've had a tough relationship. Edith had always been harsh. I rented an apartment for six weeks. That was the time she asked for and I would visit on the weekends, checking in on her. She was doing great." He looked at the ceiling. "She said she was ready to fix herself and be the wife and mother we deserve."

"How long did it last?"

"About five weeks. In February, she stopped answering my calls and when I went out there, she was gone. No note. Of all the selfish, self-destructive things she's done, why would she get pregnant and not tell me? That boy should have been here on the ranch from day one."

The horse shifted her ears, sensitive to her dad's raised voice.

Lyrissa said, "I stopped trying to figure her out long ago. It's easier to say I don't have a mother. It might be wrong, but we've got the boys now and we just need to move forward without her."

Reno patted Mundo's shoulder then gripped it. "She's right. You've got the boys. They have your last name. I don't think any court in the country would say she was a fit mother."

A heavy silence filled the air. Reno scanned the barn. There was more work needing to be done here than Mundo had let on. He had said the front fences needed some attention, but it was much deeper than a few fence posts. "Once I finish the last job, we can sit down and make a plan for your place. You know I do more than fences."

"Oh, I can't afford a full-time ranch hand."

"Good. I'm thinking a part-time gig would work out for us both."

"Aren't you taking the exam to be a fire-fighter?" Mundo asked.

Reno shrugged. "Maybe. I haven't decided." He had already tried twice and failed. The physical part he had passed with flying colors. The written part might end his dreams. Being a handyman wasn't a bad career choice for him. With his sister gone, he didn't want to run the construction company alone.

Mundo checked the last hoof then patted the mare's shoulder. "I'm going to take her out. Y'all head back to the house. Thank you for following me out and letting me process the news." He looked at his daughter. "I'm okay. This will all work out for the best. I always wanted more kids." The corner of his mouth quirked. "Not how I imagined, but it's good." He looked at his watch. "Give me an hour. I'll be back in the house ready to talk to the boys."

Mundo unlatched the lead from the post and walked past Reno. He paused and gripped his shoulder for a mere second. "I see your struggle. You're a good man. Have faith in yourself."

The hooves clicked on the brick walkway as they went out the back doors. Lyrissa came to stand by his side. "What did he say to you?"

How did the man have the heart to lift Reno when his world was crumbling? "Just some words of encouragement."

"That's my dad for you. So, you're the town's handyman and want-to-be firefighter? I always thought you were going to leave Port Del Mar and do heroic deeds."

A dry laugh, more like a *humph*, was his first response. "Yeah, well I changed my mind." He turned to head back to the house but paused and waited for her. "Are you okay? This has been a rough few days for you."

"Oh, you know. It's what one is used to if Dee-ann Herff Martinez is your mother. When can I get off this roller coaster?"

His heart dipped a little. There were no words. She had every right to hate this town and get back to the life she had created for herself in Missouri. He didn't like the silence. "So, your dad said you just finished your master's degree in special education. He's immensely proud of you. Do you have a job lined up in Missouri?"

"I did. It was temporary while I finished my master's. I ran the youth and special needs programs for a church. It was a small community and perfect for me at the time."

"With summer about to start, you probably have to get back."

She shook her head. "Did you miss the part where my mom used my key to clean out the cashbox? They have her on video. They understandably asked for the keys back and they already have someone else to run the programs. She was my intern, so it worked out for her." She sighed. "I can focus on the boys, and I have résumés out. The next few weeks, I'll send more. Location doesn't matter to me as long as it's not here or anywhere close. I'll use the summer to make sure the boys and my dad are good."

The rain started again. With jackets pulled over their heads, they ran for the back porch. "I've always loved being in the rain." Her laughter rumbled through him like the thunder that rattled the landscape.

He wanted to stop and soak it in. It wasn't good of him to be having fun on such a rotten day for her and Mundo. He reached the screen door and opened it for her. Together, they shook off the water and laid their wet jackets over the back of the rocking chairs.

She turned away and lifted the lid on a wicker storage box. Facing him again, she had two towels. Without warning, she used the soft blue towel to wipe his face. The gold flecks in her dark green eyes danced. "How is it fair that you even look good caught in the rain while I look like a drowned rat?"

"Rat? You look more like a lost mermaid." He couldn't contain his smile. "You think I'm good-looking?"

With a chuckle, she shook her head. "It's no secret in town that everyone thinks you're good-looking, so don't go getting any ideas. You're not my type. I prefer reading to partying." She stepped away and toweled off.

The light mood evaporated, and his heart went a little heavy. Someone else who wrote him off as shallow and only good for entertainment.

With a sigh, he followed her into the house. So much for clicking with her. He misread the situation as usual. Putting a smile back on his face, he joined her family.

Lyrissa was losing her mind. It was all the stress with her family. That was it. Otherwise, she would have never had the wild feeling that

she should move closer to Reno. He was the opposite of everything she wanted in her life.

Okay. So, he was cute in a very unreal way.
Hollywood would take him up the minute he
knocked on the door. But then, everything in
life came too easy for him. His carefree smile
was evidence.

He was nice and all. His family was one of the
best. A very functional family. He was the wild
child of the group but there wasn't a hint of the
dysfunction that ruled the house she grew up in.

And now, she had two brothers to add to the
mess. They needed her. Her father and grandmother needed her. No time to get all weird
around Reno Espinoza.

In the house, they found her grandmother on
the sofa. The boys had pulled out all the games
that had been stored in the TV cabinet.

"Oh, good. You're back." Her grandmother
stood. "I need to get going. Forgot how much
energy young ones have. They also have lots of
questions."

"Thank you, Mew-Maw," Lyrissa said. The
boys had pulled out all her father's favorites.
She wasn't sure if the games were age-appro-
priate for them.

"How's your father?" Mew-Maw stepped
closer and lowered her voice. "What has that
daughter of mine done now?" She glanced at

the boys. "She hates me so much she's kept my grandsons from me."

"I don't think it has anything to do with you. It's all her."

The older woman let out a dry laugh and the boys looked up from the chess pieces and stones they were playing with. She waved them off. "Don't mind me, boys. Go back to your thingies there."

She shook her head. "Lyrissa, take my word for it. She hates me. Told me so many times. The last time I told her she was out of my will. The ranch and every last speck of dirt on it was going to you and your father. Oh, man. She was furious. That was the last time she came to the ranch."

Shock rocked Lyrissa. "When did you do that? Does Daddy know?"

"Of course. I had to tell him so he wouldn't be blindsided. The ranch and most of my accounts are going to you. I love your father, but he has a weak spot for your mother. If he thought it would help her, he'd give it all away. So, I can't trust him when it comes to her. But you have a strong head on your shoulders. You won't let her take advantage of you."

Lyrissa had to laugh. "Really? You do realize she stole everything from me and walked away, leaving me with two brothers?"

"Oh, posh." She walked to the door and put her hat on her head then slipped her rain slicker on. "She used the boys to con you. You won't let that happen again. Hey, boys. I'm heading out. Y'all come over to my house tomorrow."

Ray-Ray jumped up and ran to her and threw his arms around her leg. "Bye, Mew-Maw. I always wanted a grandma and you're the best."

With a scowl on her face, she patted his back. "Easy, boy. You'll knock me over. And I don't know about being the best. I'm good with horses, not so much people. But I'm glad you and your brother made it home. This is where you belong." She nodded at Bennett. He still sat on the floor at the coffee table with a game of chess and Go scattered over the tabletop.

He didn't look as eager to have a grandmother. Now that she knew the truth, she could see her father in the boy. How had she missed it earlier? Her grandmother was right. He had the look of a Herff, but his eyes were all her father's. The shape and color.

Mew-Maw chuckled and squeezed Ray-Ray's shoulder before dislodging him. She pointed at her skeptical grandson. "That one is one hundred percent Herff. It won't hurt to smile, boy." With one last goodbye she went out the door.

Ray-Ray grabbed Lyrissa's hand and pulled her to the coffee table. Then ran to the perpet-

ually smiling Reno. Leaning against the doorframe, he looked too comfortable in the middle
of this mess of her life.

Ray-Ray picked up a thin pamphlet and handed
it to Reno. "We want to play this game with the
astronauts. Right, Benny? This one looks cool."

"That's a chessboard my father bought when
we visited NASA. We have several boards with
different themes. He is a serious player." The
memories of all the nights playing with him
brought a smile to her lips. "Have y'all played
before? He would love it if you would play with
him."

Taking Reno's hand, Ray-Ray tugged on it.
"Do you know how to play? If not, read us the
directions. I want to play chess with our grandpa.
Benny can't read. Well, he can but he stumbles
over the—"

"Stop talking. I can read. I just don't want to,"
Bennett snapped at his little brother.

Ray-Ray sighed and looked up at Reno.
"You'll read them to me?"

Reno looked at the pamphlet in his hand and
a flash of panic burned in his eyes before he
laughed. "You know what I like doing?" He
tossed the chess booklet on the sofa and sat on
the floor next to Bennett. "Making my own
rules. We don't need to read someone else's."

That was twice in less than an hour Reno had

laughed off reading something aloud. Was she just seeing signs of a learning disability because she had just studied that topic for almost two years, or was Reno hiding the fact he couldn't read?

She didn't recall it being an issue in school, but they never had classes together. Not that it was any of her business. She had enough of her own issues.

"If you're going to play with my dad, you will have to know the agreed-upon rules. He takes chess and Go very seriously." She lowered herself to the ground on the opposite side of Reno and crossed her legs. "I'll teach you the game. We'll start with chess since it's easier to learn."

Reno's eyes went wide. "Chess is the easier game?"

"Yep. We don't need the book. It's all up here." She tapped her head. "My father would love that y'all learned."

As she set up the chessboard and went over the moves, she noticed Bennett intensely studying every word and action, but if she made eye contact, he would sit back and look away. He didn't want her to see how much he wanted this.

Okay, she could pretend he didn't care. For now.

That was the attitude she should adopt with Reno. She would just pretend she didn't care and he wouldn't notice her weirdness.

Across from her, Reno was so relaxed and had both boys laughing at his mistakes. He made it okay for them to miss a step or make a wrong move. Probably because he was still a kid at heart.

She had loved her mother so much. Just one smile from her would light up Lyrissa's world. But that joy brought so much pain, eventually. Big smiles were good for a moment but couldn't be counted on in the long run.

That was the thing about people who never took life seriously. They were fun to be around. Until real problems interfered with their fun. They couldn't be counted on when they were needed.

Chapter Five

Thunder shook the house. A bolt of lightning flashed so brightly through the windows, Reno was blinded for a moment. All the lights went out.

Ray-Ray whimpered. Reno stood. "Do you know where your dad keeps the flashlights or candles?"

She reached for a drawer under the coffee table. "Here's two small ones." She turned one on and handed it to Reno. She sat the other on the worn wood. "The big lights are on top of the refrigerator. There is also an old hurricane lamp on the mantel. It should have oil in it. I hope he's in the barn and not outside."

He didn't need to see her to know she was worried about her father. It was heavy in her voice.

Lyrissa struggled to stand with Ray-Ray clinging to her neck. Moving to them, Reno gave her his hand to help her up. Before she was stable on her feet, she broke contact. He fought the need to reach out again to support her. Instead, he shoved his free hand in his pocket.

In a few steps, she put distance between them and grasped for Bennett's arm. The boy nearly stumbled when he backed into the coffee table to get away from her.

Reno handed the second flashlight to Bennett and they followed him into the kitchen. Another flash of lightning lit up the dark sky.

Her phone vibrated. It was her father. "He's going to stay in the barn until it's cleared out."

Reno nodded. "Good. That's the wisest move. This kind of storm can be dangerous."

She nodded then licked her lips.

Instinct told him to take her in his arms and reassure her. That was a huge no go, so he settled with a weak "We'll be safe in the house."

Armed with flashlights, they went back into the living room. With her free hand, she lit the hurricane lamp. The soft light glowed, illuminating her when she faced him. Her arm held the small boy close to her chest. "He wants us to go ahead and share the good news." She tried smiling but it was tight.

Reno tilted his head. "Good news?" He studied her. "Oh, news in the letter?"

"Yeah. That one."

"Is it about Momma?" For the first time, Bennett didn't even try to hide his obvious interest.

"Yes. Let's sit down." She sat on the edge of the sofa. Bennett willingly sat close to her. Reno put the lamp in the center of the coffee table then pulled up the rocking chair, so they were in a tight circle.

"Well?" Bennett's one word dripped with impatience.

"Okay. So. Your mom. Our mom had a very big surprise for Dad. It's the best surprise ever."

She pulled her lips in, then looked up to the ceiling. His heart went out to her. How did she tell one brother that he was her father's biological son, and the other wasn't?

The silence grew heavy as the boys stared at her. Anticipation bubbled from every pore.

"The best surprise ever? Really?" Bouncing on his knees, Ray-Ray leaned forward in excitement.

Her gaze sought his. Once again, she was silently pleading for his help. He wasn't going to let her down this time.

With a careful grin, Reno looked at each boy. "It *is* the best surprise *ever.*" He leaned in and scanned the room as if he had a big secret. "Mundo always wanted more kids, and your mom knows this. In the letter she granted his wish. She told Mundo that he is legally your father. His name is on both of your birth certificates. He didn't have a clue until he got the letter.

He was so excited to find out he has sons he didn't know what to do and had to go outside."

Ray-Ray leaned closer, his eyes gleaming. Bennett crossed his arms and narrowed his eyes.

"You have a father now. He happens to be Bennett's biological father. And Ray-Ray, you have his exact same name. Raymundo Jesus Martinez. You have the same name as him because she wanted you to have a real father and she knew Mundo was the best."

Bennett gazed skeptically between the two adults. "That doesn't make any sense."

Not knowing what else to do, Reno nodded. "I know. It's wild, right?" Was he getting in over his head? He looked to Lyrissa for support. She pulled Ray-Ray closer to her and nodded at him to continue. She wasn't ready to take over.

Faking confidence, Reno smiled. The boys had been lied to enough. But how to handle this very complicated truth in a way a child would understand? How much truth was too much?

With a big sigh, he gave himself a bit of time to organize the words. "It can be super confusing. But here it is." Leaning forward, he held out his hands as if explaining the next play in a football game. "There are a few different types of fathers. One—a biological father. That's the guy who knows your mom and you get your DNA from him. Then there's a real father who raises you. He's there for you whenever you need him. He takes you to school, goes to your events and gives you advice. Sometimes the biological father and the real father are the same man. But it's not always the case. What matters is that from this day on and forever, Mundo is your real father. He's the man who will raise you and will call you both sons."

Ray-Ray jumped up. "I prayed for a father. I did but I want my mom too. Why can't we have both?"

Lyrissa reached out for him and pulled him back into her lap. She wrapped her arms around him and held him close. "Our mom lives in a world of her own making and doesn't always do the right thing for the people she loves."

"Like taking all your stuff without asking?" Ray-Ray asked.

"Yep. She makes decisions that we don't understand. I know from my own experiences that Mundo is the best father you can have. Mom is unpredictable. She wanted to keep you to herself for as long as she could, but I'm thankful and so is our dad that she wanted you to come to the ranch. That's why she finally told him the truth."

"Why didn't she tell him or us before?" Bennett's voice was low and dripping with suspicion.

They all turned to Lyrissa. Reno could see her heart breaking.

She took Bennett's hand. "Honestly, I don't know. What I do know, she has given you and our father a great gift today. She's given you a father who I promise will never leave you. I'm your big sister. We are a forever family."

Ray-Ray had tears in his eyes. He laid his head against her chest. "Promise? Because I always wanted to belong to a family with a house and a bed and a dog. Do we have a dog?"

Lyrissa chuckled. "If you ask real nice, I imagine you can get a dog."

She kissed the top of his head. Bennett shifted to the side and looked out the window.

Reno slid to the other end of the sofa and put a hand on the boy's shoulder. "You okay, Bennett? It's a lot to take in." He looked down at the small hands and tight fists.

Bennett wipe his nose with the back of his hand. "There's been a couple of guys that mom said we could call dad." He shrugged. "They didn't stick around. Which wasn't a bad thing. They…weren't nice." He hesitated over the last words.

Lyrissa pulled him closer to her other side. She had her arms wrapped around both boys, trying to hold them all together. "This is not the same thing. He is your legal father, and he wants you here in his life. He had a bedroom waiting for you."

"He did." Ray-Ray's eyes were wide and full of wonder.

Bennett pulled away from her and moved closer to him.

His heart fluttered at the sign of growing trust. "Bennett, listen to me. Those other men were not the same thing at all." He nudged Bennett with his shoulder. "I lost my dad when I was a young kid like you."

Ray-Ray popped up. "Was he your real dad or your biological dad?"

With a soft laugh, Reno nodded. "He was both and when I lost him, I thought I had lost everything. My sister's friend—" he nodded to Lyrissa "—your sister—had a cool dad. I would follow my sister here and hang out with Mundo. He always made the time to talk to me. I still find reasons to come over once a week. There is not a man who would love being your father more than Mundo."

The back door slammed.

Ray-Ray jumped up from her lap. When Mundo walked into the living room, the small boy hurled himself at his new father. "Are you really my dad forever? No takebacks?"

A large, calloused hand came around him and held him close. "I am." Mundo ran his free hand through his wet hair. His voice was raw. He nodded to Bennett, who sat stiffly on the sofa, arms crossed.

"I pray you can open your hearts and allow me to make up for lost time."

Reno's skin was too tight. The family needed time together and he needed to breathe. He stood. "I need to get to the firehouse. Volunteers are needed to clear roads and check on people. Y'all have a good evening."

If he stayed, he would start imagining being part of this family too, being a real part of Lyrissa's life. But she made it clear her life was not here and even if it was, he was not her type.

Lyrissa bit back the plea for Reno to stay. With her dad on the sofa next to Bennett and Ray-Ray on his lap, she followed Reno to the door. "Thank you for everything. It's been an overwhelming day. You helped us get through it." She tilted her head. He really had.

"I'm always here to bring a smile. That's what I'm good at." He stood on the porch and for a second just studied her.

Self-conscious, she tucked loose strands behind her ear. "Well, I appreciate it. Be careful out there."

She stayed on the porch until he was out of sight. It would be so easy to get mixed up with the charming Reno Espinoza again. Not that they even made it to their first date the last time, but still.

Her father's laughter came through the door. What was she thinking? She had a family with major healing ahead of them. There was also the matter of finding a job. One as far from Port Del Mar as possible. Mooning over Reno was just avoiding the real issues.

As soon as her father and brothers were settled, she would be gone.

Chapter Six

Reno dodged a large rut, but hit a smaller one. The Herff Ranch drive really needed work. All the effort and money had gone into keeping the production part of the ranch working. It wouldn't hurt to spend a little time on the aesthetics.

He had planned to come out Friday, but he'd finished the other job a day early. So here he was. Next to him sat a welcome dinner from his mom. She had asked him to drop it off. It was a good reason to be here.

And he was a big old liar. When his mom asked if he had the time to take it, he jumped at the chance to come back out. What he should have said was that he had to do a bid on a kitchen and bath extension on another ranch. He re-scheduled.

Construction wasn't as fun now that his sister was gone. She loved detailed woodwork. He was good at putting things together but didn't have the creative eyes she had. And when it came to the bookkeeping, he really missed her.

Now that she was gone, he should just go back to being a ranch hand. Before starting the business with his sister, he had worked full-time at the Wimberlys' ranch. He was good at that.

It didn't look as if his dream of being a firefighter was ever going to happen. There was no way he'd pass the written exam.

His mother would be happy. She hated the idea of him being a first responder. She didn't even like that he volunteered.

His big brother was in law enforcement and a few years back he had been shot in the line of duty. It had brought Bridges home, but his mother also used every opportunity to encourage them to find another line of work. Tapping her chest, she would tell them how much her heart worried.

He grinned. She was small, with the heart of a warrior. But she wasn't above emotional blackmail to keep her children safe and close by.

Before he brought his truck to a complete stop, Lyrissa ran out from behind the house, waving at him. He jumped out of the truck. "What's wrong?"

"I can't find the boys. Mew-Maw and Dad went into town. The boys and I went to check on the stock tank. They wanted to come back to the house to get something to eat. They're not here. I went to the barns. Buster, the horse Ray-Ray was riding, is back at the barn with all his gear on. Reno, they don't understand all the dangers on the ranch."

Her gaze darted around the yard. "I should have come back with them, but I wanted to check on the... Ray-Ray!" She sprinted to the large side gate. The youngest boy was running to them. His face was red, and wet with tears.

"Benny is stuck. We..." He couldn't get any more words out. Reno was right behind Lyrissa. She fell to her knees in the muddy pasture and pulled Ray-Ray to her.

"Take a breath." He put a hand on the boy's shoulder. "Where's Bennett?" He had his phone out, ready to call dispatch if needed.

The boy rubbed his eyes and took several breaths. "We wanted to help Mew-Maw. Before getting a snack, we rode along the fence lines like she told us about. We wanted to help."

Lyrissa cupped his face, using her thumbs to wipe at the tears. "Is he with the horse?"

Ray-Ray nodded. "We...we slipped into a huge crack in the ground. It was muddy. I landed on the top side. My horse jumped up and ran away. Benny's slipped down on its back. He told me to...to stay on the top and he went to help the horse. It was on its back and couldn't stand up."

Worst-case scenarios ran through Reno's head. A panicked thousand-pound animal with hooves was a dangerous situation for an experienced horseman. A small kid with no knowledge was not good.

"Can you take us to him? How far away is he?"

Ray-Ray pointed in the direction he came from. "I went through a gate and climbed a fence."

"He's in the bottom fifty. There's a washed-out ravine on the edge. A four-wheeler would be the fastest way there." Her words were rushed as she ran to the barn. Reno picked up the small boy and followed her.

At the largest barn, she reached inside the door and tossed him a key. "You know where we're going?"

She reached for her brother. "You take the single. It's faster." He nodded as he handed Ray-Ray over to her.

"I'll follow with him in the Coleman. It'll be safer."

He didn't hesitate. Time could make all the difference for Bennett in a situation like this. Helmet on, he didn't look back. As he went through the gates, he left them open.

Once in the last pasture, it didn't take long to spot the horse. All four legs were in the air. Deep grooves were slashed into the soft dirt around him. His head was to the side. He was breathing heavily from exhaustion from the struggle.

Reno's heart squeezed as he scanned the area for the boy.

He eased to the edge of the grass line. "Bennett?" He kept his voice low and steady. The horse tried to lift its head.

"Reno?"

Relief flooded his system at the sound of that sweet voice.

"Where's Ray-Ray? Is he okay?" The ragged voice came from under the horse.

"Yes. He found us. He's safe with Lyrissa. They're on a slower ATV. Are you okay?"

There was a narrow ditch under the horse. Bennett must be there. "I tried to help Smokey get—" a sob interrupted his words "—up, but I slipped and fell in. He reared then landed on top. I'm flat in the mud." His voice broke. "I'm sorry. We wanted—" Sniffles stopped him this time.

"I know this is scary, but I need you to relax. I called the firehouse. They have equipment that helps rescue big animals. You'd be amazed how many times this kind of stuff happens out here. We're going to get you and Smokey out, but I need you to stay calm and be still. Can you do that?"

"Yes."

"Benny?" Ray-Ray had jumped from the larger ATV and was running when Lyrissa caught up to him and picked him up.

"Shhh. We are going to get him up. But we don't want to spook the horse." She cradled his head against her shoulder. Her eyes went to Reno, silently pleading for good news.

"He's in a crevice under Smokey. He doesn't seem to be hurt, just trapped." He didn't need to mention what could go wrong. "I called it in. One of us needs to be at the house to lead them out here. They have the gear to pull up the horse. If we go down in the muddy slope we could just make it worse."

She nodded, then hugged Ray-Ray. "The firemen are coming to help. We need to go meet them so we can show them how to get here. Okay?"

Nodding, he leaned away from her. "Benny?"

"Yeah." The voice was a little shaky, but Reno was impressed by how well the kid was doing. "I'm good. I got a comfy little spot. I just need someone to help get Smokey so I can come out. Reno said the firemen are coming with trucks."

Lyrissa patted the small boy in her arms. "Ray-Ray and I are going to meet the firemen. Then I'm fixing a big lunch for everyone."

Once they left for the house, Reno lay on his stomach and studied the area. He talked in a low, soothing voice to help keep the boy and horse calm.

Time crawled. Finally, the rumbling of the

big rescue truck sounded at the pasture gate. "They're here. We'll have you out soon." He prayed that he spoke the truth.

He knew everyone in the crew except one young guy. But Reno was focused on getting Bennett out and didn't do more than give the teen a passing glance. They discussed the problem and the best way to get the horse up without risk to the boy. With expertise, they gently maneuvered the large straps under the horse.

Lyrissa and Ray-Ray were back, but they stayed on the ATV. About twenty minutes into getting everything in place and checking for safety, another truck approached them. It was Mundo and Edith. They wanted to help, but he told them the best way to help was to stay out of the way.

The crew started pulling the horse up and Reno slid into place to grab Bennett as soon as he was clear. The horse was on solid ground, shaking but standing.

With Bennett in his arms, Reno came up the slippery slope with the help of one of the guys. Another group of first responders were carefully removing the wide yellow straps from the dazed horse.

"That was amazing." With a laugh, the teen slapped Smokey on the rump.

Startled and stressed, the horse reared and

twisted. Reno saw a flash of hoof before he turned to shield the boy with his body. The impact knocked him to the ground. The horse jumped over him and ran. Someone was yelling at the teen. Apparently, his name was Devin.

"Are you okay?" he asked the boy cradled under him.

"Yes?" The small voice lacked confidence. Standing, Reno adjusted the boy's weight. Pain shot through him, and his sight went blurry. *Oh man, I'm going to faint. Not cool.*

Lyrissa's heart stopped the moment that teenager slapped Smokey's rump. It didn't matter how gentle a horse was; everyone knew to not startle them when they were in flight mode.

Watching the horse rear up on its hind legs then lunge and kick out toward Bennett's small form stopped her heart. She knew she would never be fast enough to protect him. But Reno was. He had shielded her brother with his body and took the blow.

When he stood up so fast, all the tension had flooded from her limbs. The relief had been overwhelming, but short-lived as Reno crumbled back toward the ground.

The crew surrounded Reno. One of the EMTs brought Bennett to her and said he was good, but they needed to take Reno in. Edith loaded the boys into the truck and took them to the house while she and her father followed with the four-wheelers.

She prayed it wasn't a head injury. It had happened so fast. She wanted to stay and make sure he was going to be okay, but for now all she could do was focus on the boys.

They needed to address the fact that they thought it was a good idea to go out to the pastures by themselves. She knew they were scared. So was she. And guilty for letting them out of her sight. Now Reno was in trouble, and it was her family's fault.

She prayed all the way back to the house.

Her father sat them all down at the kitchen table and talked calmly about the day. In all the excitement of the boys moving in, they had forgotten to establish rules and expectations.

So, a list was made and hung in the kitchen. The boys kept asking about Reno. There was a great deal of guilt to go around.

"I'll call his sister." Gathered at the table, not eating the lunch she had made, everyone stared at her as she spoke with Resa.

"A broken clavicle and dislocated shoulder caused him to pass out. The doctors are discussing if he needs surgery. There is no indication of a head injury."

"That's good." Her throat was so tight it was hard to speak.

"Reno's worried about Bennett. He keeps asking for you too. Can you come and reassure him you're all okay?"

She glanced at her father and grandmother. Mundo nodded. "Go. We'll keep the boys."

It didn't take her long to cross the bridge and enter the hospital.

Room number in hand, she tried to steady her breathing. Each step closer to his room tightened her nerves. She wasn't sure why she was having a hard time breathing.

Taking a deep breath, she tapped on the door to his room. His mother opened it with a wide smile. "*Pásenle. Pásenle. Como esta?*"

Lyrissa nodded at the invitation. "I'm good. *Muy bien.* Thank you."

His mother, barely five feet tall, stepped back then leaned in closer to her and whispered, "He is asking for you. He is also heavily medicated so he's not making much sense." She made her way to the side of the hospital bed.

The room was full of people. His oldest sister, Margarita, and her husband stood on the other side of the bed with Resa. If she remembered correctly, she was a midwife. His brother, Bridges, was in some sort of law enforcement uniform. There were a few people who looked familiar, but she couldn't place them.

A couple of kids sat in the window playing a card game. There wasn't much room left. Reno was in the center, asleep. A sling was over his left shoulder and supported his arm.

"I'm sorry. I'll come back later. I brought these for him." The boys had picked out snacks to give him. She had grabbed a couple of magazines—one about coastal fishing and the other about cows and horses. She laid them at the foot of the bed then backed away, moving toward the door.

"Oh, no, no, no." His mother stopped her. "You stay. Some of us were leaving." She waved her hands around.

Reno opened his eyes and groaned. Everyone in the room stopped midmovement and looked at him.

"Lyr...issa?" His voice was thick and rough.

"She's right here." His tiny mother pulled her to the side of the bed, forcing his sisters to move out of the way.

He blinked, then searched the room as if lost. She was standing on the side of his uninjured arm, so she reached out and laid her hand over his. "Reno. We can't thank you enough for protecting Bennett."

"Ben... Bennen." His long lashes went down.

Had he gone back to sleep? Then they opened wide and he blinked rapidly. "Bennett? Is…" His words slurred but she was pretty sure he was asking if her brother was okay.

"Not a scratch on him, thanks to your quick move. He just needed a good shower to wash off the mud. You saved him. Thank you."

"You good? Was worried." His lids went down again.

Leaning forward, she smiled at him and pushed back an unruly curl from his forehead. "I'm great. All is good on the Herff-Martinez home front, thanks to you."

"You're lovely. So pretty." He mumbled some other sounds, but his mouth didn't seem capable of forming legible words. His grin was lopsided as he reached out to touch her face.

Stunned, she didn't move. Was he actually flirting while banged up in the hospital?

"Easy, boy." His brother was on the opposite side of the bed. Extending his tall frame across the bed, Bridges eased Reno's good arm back to his bedside.

Reno frowned. "Want to…" More random sounds came from his lips. "Pretty."

There were a few soft giggles around the room.

She wasn't sure what to do. "Reno, I brought a couple of magazines, and the boys wanted you to have good snacks."

He lifted his hand again and cupped her face. "You the best." Narrowing his eyes, he shook his head. "I... I..." His gaze left hers and went around the room. "Why you all here?"

His mother stepped forward. The worry was still in her face. She covered his right foot with her hand. "You were hurt. We're here to make sure you have everything you need."

He glared at her. "I'm not a baby." Turning back to Lyrissa, he winced, obviously in pain, but then gave her a wide, goofy grin. "I have a sec..." He closed his eyes. "Secret."

Opening them, he leaned forward. "Come here," he slurred.

With trepidation, she moved closer. He flung his good arm out and wrapped it around her neck. "Only you to know." The words ran together.

"Hey, champ." His brother intervened again. "No mauling your guest." He pulled his arm off Lyrissa and gently pushed him back into the pillow.

"But I love her." That came out way too clearly.

A cold sweat broke out over her whole body. She looked around the room at the amused faces. "We're just friends. Really. I have no idea why he is saying these things."

"I say these things because they are the truth." His head rolled back, and his eyes closed.

Heat climbed up her neck. *Please let him fall asleep.* "On that note, I think it's time for me to go."

His hand reached out and touched her fingers. "Sorry." He looked around. "I need paper...pen."

One of his older nephews grabbed his backpack and pulled out the supplies he needed. "Thank you, Coop." Struggling to hold the pen, he stuck out his tongue. "I can't spell good."

"*G-o-o-d,*" a small niece offered. A few chuckles filled the room.

He squinted one eye at her. "Not what I meant, but okay." He went back to focusing on his note. "There." He handed it to Lyrissa.

Bridges went to take it and Reno pulled back. "Nope. I'm doing this...with...without my family. You do everything for me. I'm tired of being an Es... Espa." He grunted. "I am a grown man and I don't want to be an Espino...za. That's a hard word. I was in the...fourth grade before I spelt it. *Reno* is easy." He nodded then closed his eyes. "I'm just Reno from now on."

His mother put a hand to her chest. "*Mijo,* what's wrong? I've never heard you say such things before. You could spell your name in first grade."

"Nope. Maddy and Crystal wrote it for me. They took my spelling test too. I can't spell or read." He pressed his finger to his lips. "Shhhh.

Don't tell. It's a secret 'cause I don't you to be diss...dissa...p...p...worry. Don't worry."

Lyrissa looked from him to his mom. The poor woman had tears in her eyes. Resa went to her side and wrapped an arm around her shoulder. "Mom. Don't let anything he says worry you. He is heavily medicated and doesn't know what he is saying."

"But all this about reading and spelling makes no sense. He passed all his classes."

"Mom. We'll figure it out later. He's going to be okay."

"Okay," Reno said, louder than needed. "Ever since trapped in the box you worried about me. No more worry. No more. I'm..." He blinked as if he forgot what he was saying. He held up the note. "This is for you. Only you." He glared at his brother.

Bridges lifted his hand in surrender. "I was only trying to save you from yourself. I'm thinking you might regret whatever is in that note once the painkillers wear off, little brother."

Reno blew out a hard puff of air. "I don't need you or you or you or you." His gaze went around the room. "To save me. Here." Once again he handed the note to Lyrissa.

With a weak attempt at a smile, she took it from him. She had always thought the Espinozas were the perfect family. Apparently, there were some undercurrents in the calm waters. She really didn't want to be here.

Looking at the note, she bit her bottom lip. Maybe once the drugs wore off, he'd forget he gave it to her. That would be for the best. No need to embarrass herself or him.

"Read it. Please." His gaze was so earnest as he watched her. The room was dead silent.

The back of the page was facing her. If she didn't turn it over, she would not have to deal with any of his drug-induced secrets.

"What do you say?" he asked, his voice clearer than before.

"I don't know." It was all she could offer.

He blinked. "You don't know? That's not an ans…answer. Yes or no?"

"What did you ask her?" Bridges put all of his authority as an officer and older brother into the short question.

With an exasperated sigh, Reno flopped back onto his pillow. The pain brought his right hand to his left shoulder.

Gently, she laid her hand on top of his. "This is not the time to talk about it. Focus on getting better than we'll talk. In private."

His mouth opened and he scanned the room and if surprised that they had an audience. He leaned forward. "Right." He nodded. Then he closed his eyes. "Bennett's safe?"

"Yes. Thank you for saving him. If there is anything we can do to repay you, let us know."

"No. He's a good kid…just wanted to help with ranch work."

"I know. I'll check on you later. Bye." She stepped away before he could say anything more. A quick trip to the hospital had turned into a complicated mess.

She rushed out of the room. She knew she was being rude, but she didn't want anyone to ask her questions about the note.

Once she was alone in her car, she took a deep breath then turned the paper over. *WIL U MARY M?*

Her heart stopped. Why would he ask her that, even in a drug-induced state? It was so far from anything she knew how to handle. This was not real. He wasn't in his right mind. Once the meds wore off, he'd have no memory of this.

She wouldn't bring it up, saving both of them from the humiliation of this bizarre question.

On another subject, it was obvious his family had no clue he was dyslexic. It wasn't uncommon for an undiagnosed student to figure out strategies to hide it. They didn't understand there was help. Without being exposed to learning disabilities, they would just think something was wrong with them and work to hide it.

Apparently, no one in his family had dealt

with it so he had been on his own and solved the problem the best way he could. This was her area of expertise, but after so many years of hiding it, she worried he would not be open to letting her help him.

There were so many ways dyslexia presented. She knew she could assist him, if he'd accept it.

She looked at the note, then carefully folded the paper and put it in her bag. She was nowhere close to being his type and he was the last person she would want in her life. It didn't matter, anyway. She would be leaving soon. He wasn't serious about wanting to marry her. She knew firsthand people were not reliable when on drugs, any kind of drug.

She thought back to their first day here and how Reno had stepped in and helped. She shook her head. Really, where had that proposal come from?

Chapter Seven

Sweat beaded Reno's forehead and it wasn't from the heat. The Martinez house loomed before him. If the gossip from his siblings, nephews and nieces were to be believed, he had made a total fool of himself in front of Lyrissa.

They loved reminding him how he had pulled her over and declared his undying love. He swallowed. They had to be exaggerating. *Please, God. Let them be tall tales with little to no truth.*

They said he also had declared he remembered everything about the day he was trapped in a box on the fishing boat. And because he was on a roll to clear out all his secrets, he admitted he couldn't read or write and had cheated to get through school.

Lyrissa had been there to hear it all. Slamming his head against the steering wheel, he let out a groan. He was going to have legal papers drawn up that none of his family members were ever allowed to be around him in a hospital until he was fully aware.

Not that it mattered now. Every secret he had worked so hard to keep hidden from his family over the years was out. His mother kept crying. Apologizing for being neglectful and missing the signs.

Leaning back in the truck, he closed his eyes and prayed. Prayed for God's wisdom and peace. The past week had been all about trying to get the smile back on his mother's face.

He hated that she felt responsible for any of his faults. That had been the whole reason he had hidden them for so long. She didn't deserve to cry another tear in her life.

Now he had to face Lyrissa and try to put all the toothpaste back in the tube. She had no interest in him, and he knew that. He valued her friendship and didn't want it to be awkward or weird between them.

Plus, the idea that she now knew he couldn't read or write was downright embarrassing. She had a master's degree in education, and he barely got out of high school. Yeah, she'd really want to hang out and have deep conversations with him.

His favorite things to talk about were ranch stuff, movies and fishing. She was probably one of those people who preferred the book over the movie. He reached for the key to turn the engine back on and back out before anyone saw him. One more week would be good.

"Reno!" Ray-Ray launched out of the front door, waving and jumping. Bennett, much more aloof, followed.

Caught. He turned off the engine, opened the door and stepped out, remembering not to use his left side.

"Reno!" Ray-Ray turned to look behind him. "Dad! Reno's here!"

The small boy ran to Reno and stopped a foot away. "Can I hug you? Is it hurt bad? It was so scary to see the horse go up and knock you down. But you twisted like Spider-Man and saved Benny." He spun his little body then threw his head back with his hands clutching his chest. "Then you passed out. I was so scared. Are you better? Dad said we couldn't go to the hospital. That you needed to rest. I made you a drawing. It's in the house."

"Whoa there, boy." Mundo braced his hands on the shoulders of Ray-Ray and laughed. "As you can hear, Ray-Ray has been very worried about you." His smile dimmed a little. "It was a traumatic day for him and his brother."

"I'm okay," Bennett grumbled. He eyed Reno with curiosity but hung back with his arms crossed. "Are you okay? That horse was big."

Reno went to one knee. "My shoulder took a little hit and needs to rest a bit, but I'm good. You and your brother were so brave. I'm proud of the way you stayed cool the whole time under the horse and told your brother to go get help. It's okay if you need to talk about it. When I was younger, I was once trapped in a fishing boat box all day. I didn't know if I would make it home. Sometimes, I still have dreams about the darkness and the waves. So, if you get scared, it's okay to talk to your dad or sister." He knew how hard it was to hold it in and suffer alone.

"He can talk to me too." Ray-Ray jumped up and down.

"That's good advice, Reno." Lyrissa joined them. The morning sun kissed her skin and reflected the red streaks in her dark hair. For a moment, he forgot to breathe. She was so beautiful.

He stood, making sure to fill his lungs. That thought had to be banished from his head. Today was about convincing her that anything he said in the hospital had to be forgotten.

With one smile from her, the songbirds sounded happier. He was still on painkillers. To make sure he didn't say anything stupid, he kept silent.

Lyrissa knelt in front of Bennett. "Being brave doesn't mean you don't get scared."

With a nod, Reno agreed with her. "I'll give you my number. You can call or text anytime. Nighttime can be the hardest. If you don't want to wake anyone, I'm always up late." He held the boy's gaze until he got a nod. "I was sent to deliver a homemade meal from my mother's kitchen. It might include brownies. Anyone want to help me take it in?"

Ray-Ray lifted his hand. "Me! I want to help."

Laughing, Mundo patted him on the shoulder. "Come on, son. We'll take care of it." With Lyrissa's father guiding the boys, the containers were taken into the house.

"Thank you. Not just for saving him, but for opening up and giving him someone to talk to. I understand you don't talk about the time you were trapped. Savannah had told me the story back in high school. All those hours lost were terrifying for them. They had thought it a blessing you didn't remember." She pulled her lips in then glanced at him through her lashes. "But you did remember. You were four?"

He nodded. It had become a habit to keep it buried and not talk about it when others retold the story from their perspective.

"Were you in the box the whole time?"

"Yes." His mouth went dry. Clearing his throat, he thought of what words to use. This was hard but it was better than talking about his attraction to her. "The inside was rough wood with the smell of wet towels and saltwater. There was a thin crack of light. The waves made me sick to my stomach. I was afraid the men on the boat would be mad at me. Somewhere in my brain, I thought they would throw me overboard. Probably something to do with the stories my older siblings told me. I prayed that I would be good and never make my mother mad or sad if God took me home to her." One corner of his mouth pulled up. He'd forgotten that part.

"You pretended not to remember to keep everyone happy?"

He shrugged then touched his left shoulder. "I guess. Whenever anyone brought it up, my mother would cry and hug me so tight I couldn't breathe."

"I'm grateful you said something. Keeping that kind of experience buried had to be hard. I wouldn't want that kind of burden for Bennett or any child. Thank you for sharing with him."

"I'm glad I could help. On the other hand, now my mother is back to tearing up every time she sees me. I had to get away. Plus, I wanted to talk to you."

There. He said it. Now he just needed to form the next words. They were all jumbled, just like when he tried to read or write. He hated it when words played hide-and-seek in his head. What was wrong with his brain?

She glanced at him then turned away. Swallowing, he tried searching for the right words. He had already embarrassed himself enough.

Just a simple apology. But he should say what he was apologizing for. That's where it was foggy.

"Lyrissa—"

"Uhm. Reno—"

They spoke at the same time. He adjusted his sling as they both gave an awkward chuckle. "Well, I guess that establishes that we both know each other's names."

With a grin, she looked at him then cut her gaze to the pasture on the other side of the drive. A herd of Herefords grazed peacefully. Bringing her gaze back to him, she smiled unnaturally.

He opened his mouth and jumped in. "I hear from not-so-reliable sources that I might have made a fool of myself. I hope anything I said didn't make you uncomfortable." Now he was studying the cattle like his life depended on them. His skin had never felt so hot.

"You were on some pretty strong painkillers. Do you remember any of it?"

"Not a bit. And I mean that." He grinned. "It's not me pretending to avoid making you unhappy."

"There was something I really wanted to talk to you about, but I don't want to offend you."

He blew out a puff of air. "I'm pretty insult-proof. You can say anything. Please." He laid his good hand over his heart. Her taking the lead in the conversation would be so much easier than him trying to muddle through.

"Before the accident, I noticed you used some classic strategies to avoid reading aloud. In the hospital you admitted to not being able to read or write."

His nerves pinched his stomach. Maybe letting her take the lead had not been the rescue he thought. His muscles locked in place. "I can. Sometimes it's harder than other times."

"I hope I'm not overstepping, but do you or have you ever been diagnosed with dyslexia or dysgraphia?"

He just stared at her.

She bit the corner of her mouth. "Okay. I'm assuming not, since your mother was surprised by your comment. Is this why you haven't taken the written exam to be a firefighter?" She relaxed her face and tried to smile. Then she blinked a couple of times. This time she allowed the silence to hang between them.

"I don't see letters backward." Taking a deep breath, he shook his head. "I've never even heard the term *dysgraphia*. It was just hard to read or write. I can, but…" Did he tell her the truth about the exam? No one wanted to look like an idiot.

She leaned closer to him. "It's so much more complicated than backward letters. You know my specialty is working with neurodivergent students. I might be able to help. If you want me to." She held her hands up. "But like I said, it's completely up to you."

"What if we find out I'm not neurodivergent, just stu—"

"Stop. Without going any further, I can guarantee you have a solid—if not high—IQ. You figured out how to pass your classes. You speak two languages fluently. You solve problems quickly even in stressful situations. What some people don't understand is that neurodivergences just help us understand that some people have a different way to process information. Even the way they think and behave can be different."

She looked him straight in the eye. "Not wrong. Different. With support and strategies, their ways of thinking and seeing information can be a great advantage."

He raised his eyebrows.

Her voice had gotten louder. Straightening her spine, she took a breath. "Sorry. I get passionate about this and might go overboard. But the one thing I want you to know is you're in no way less than. Just different than. And that can be a good thing once identified. Your quick thinking saved my brother. If you want to be a first responder, I want to help you get there."

He tried to process everything she just said. It was overwhelming, but one thing he understood was she thought he could pass the test. "Okay. The thing is, I did take the written exam and I failed. Twice. The second time more than the first."

"On the second test. Did you get in your head?"

"What do you mean?" His chest hurt. It was strange talking about this with someone. After a lifetime of pretending it wasn't a problem, it was hard to put his doubts and struggles into words.

"Did you go into the second test doubting your ability to pass? Were you afraid you were just wasting time and money?"

A dry laugh escaped. "I did waste time and money. What's the point? I'm a good ranch hand. I'm going back to that as soon as my shoulder is better."

"You were focused on your fear instead of what you knew." She stepped closer and touched his arm. "I can help. That's what I'm trying to tell you. Let me help. Together, we can get you to pass that test. If that's what you want."

His breath was coming in short pants, like he'd ran five fast miles. Could this really happen? "You think I can pass the test?"

"Yes." She stepped closer and placed one soft hand on his shoulder. "You keep adjusting your sling. Is it hurting? We should sit." Her gaze moved up until it met his. They both froze.

The world faded away. Her face was clear and sharp. He glanced at her lips.

Yeah. He had said everything his family accused him of.

It was all in his heart, but his head knew there was no point. He leaned closer. His mouth was dry. She didn't pull away.

A hammer pinged his brain. What was he doing? She would never be his, even for a brief time. The best he could hope for was friendship and he was about to mess that up too.

Stepping back, he lost her touch. A part of him screamed to step back into her circle but the practical side won. "Sorry. It is hurting."

He hadn't even noticed he was messing with his shoulder. She pointed to the porch. He nodded and they walked up the stoop.

Settling into one of the old rockers, he became uncomfortable again. It wasn't his shoulder this time. Should he mention the hospital and beg her to forget anything he had said? Had she noticed he almost kissed her?

"Reno. I really hope you accept my help, but we also need to talk about the other thing that happened at the hospital."

His heart jumped three notches. *No.*

It was his problem, not hers. He should just jump in and take the lead. "They said I gave you a note, but no one knows what I wrote. A little

painkiller and I started making things up." He
gave her a grin, but this was what he dreaded
most. "I'm sure it was gibberish." *Please let it
be gibberish.*

She crossed her arms and sat back in her rocking chair. Her gaze was on the land around them.
With a big sigh, she turned her head. "The thing
is—"

"Lyrissa!" Ray-Ray banged the door open.
"Mew-Maw fell down. She was yelling at Momma
on the phone. And then—."

She didn't wait for Ray-Ray to finish. Reno
was right with her. In the kitchen, he went to his
knees next to Mew-Maw. Using the counter, she
supported herself when the blood stopped flowing to her legs. Her grandmother was limp on
the floor. Her head was in her father's lap.

"They were yelling at each other then she
just collapsed like in slow motion." Worry was
etched in every line of her father's face.

Reno placed his fingers on her throat. "Call
911." He counted. "Her pulse is good. Edith, can
you hear me?"

She turned her head and groaned. Lyrissa's
heart jumped in relief.

"Did she hit her head when she fell?" Reno
asked as he gently checked her.

"No." Her father's attention was fully on his

mother-in-law. "I had time to break her fall. I was moving to take the phone because the yelling got louder."

Dispatch answered. It was Izzie. Lyrissa made herself focus on giving her the information. But she couldn't take her gaze off Reno and Mew-Maw.

"Edith?" Reno's voice was gentle but firm as he touched the weathered cheek.

Her eyes blinked. "What?" Her blue gaze was unfocused.

She was awake. Lyrissa breathed for the first time since coming through the door.

"Can you tell me where you are and the last thing you remember?" Reno asked.

"I'm in Mundo's house. About to have dinner with my boys. Dee called." She closed her eyes. "That girl is going to be the death of me. I can't believe the things she said."

She was getting upset again. Reno redirected her. "It's okay. Focus on Lyrissa and the boys." He pointed to her. Ray-Ray was holding her free hand. "They're all good."

"Yes. Those boys should have been here as soon as they were born." Her voice went up. "Lyrissa, are you talking to her?" She was yelling again. Fighting Reno and her father as she struggled to get up. "Why am I on the floor?"

"You passed out. We need to make sure you're okay." Reno took her hand. "She called 911."

"Hogwash. I'm fit as a fiddlin' frog." She pointed to Lyrissa. "You had better not have called the ambulance, young lady. I don't need no one making a fuss over me. And it cost too much money."

Bennett moved a chair close to her, and Mundo helped Reno get her into it. She waved them off. "Girl, hang up that phone."

Lyrissa ignored her. She turned away so she could focus on the call. "Yes. She's alert. Thank you, Izzie." She slipped the phone into her back pocket. "The ambulance is already halfway here. She said if you don't want treatment, you have to sign a refusal form."

"I'm not going to be taken out on a stretcher like some old feeble person. Why did you call them?" She glared.

"I asked her to." Reno winked at her grandmother as if they were partners in crime. "A distraction from you lying lifeless on the floor."

Mundo moved to the counter and gave Lyrissa a look like she was the one who had to handle the older lady's stubbornness.

With a sigh, she went to one knee and took her grandmother's hand. "Mew-Maw, you were unconscious. I didn't want to waste time if it was a stroke or your heart. The boys were scared."

The older woman softened and patted Ray-

Ray's hand. "They think because I'm old, I'm going to just drop dead. I promise you boys, it's going to take much more than your mother's shenanigans to do any real damage to this old bird."

Mundo slid into the chair at the front of the table. He gave a pointed look at his daughter.

Lyrissa nodded and sat next to her grandmother. She knew a fight was coming. "We'll make an appointment with Dr. Villa as soon as his office opens."

"I ain't going to no doctor either. They just find things wrong with you and order drugs. Then they make you come back all the time."

Reno smiled at her as if all was great. "You know you're not going to the doctor for yourself," he said as his gaze met Lyrissa's. "It's for your family's peace of mind. They have enough to worry about."

Edith crossed her arms and harrumphed. "They'll want to start me on drugs. I ain't doing it."

Lyrissa wanted to beat her head against the wooden table. "Stop being so stubborn." There was a vehicle pulling up to the house. "That's the ambulance. I'll go meet them."

Reno stood as if going with her.

She pointed to the chair he had been sitting in. "Sit. I've got it." After their encounter on the porch, keeping distance between them was the best choice. She did not look at him as she left.

Right now, she was too fragile to deal with any of those weird feelings.

Brenda and Joe were at the door, and she led them to the kitchen.

Reno had everyone laughing when Lyrissa walked in with the paramedics. Even Bennett couldn't hide a half grin. Reno was in his old familiar role of jokester. Lyrissa gave him a quick glare then focused on her grandmother.

Did he ever take anything seriously?

Brenda checked on Edith as the older woman grumbled through the whole routine about people treating her like a cracked egg.

Smiling, Brenda explained what she was doing and what they were looking for. True to her word, Edith refused to go to the hospital and signed the form.

"Mew-Maw, first thing in the morning we're calling to make you an appointment. No arguments."

"I'm not a child." The woman crossed her arms over her chest. "Y'all wasted your time coming out. Sorry they bothered you."

"It was no bother, ma'am," Brenda said with a smile.

As Lyrissa walked the pair out, Reno was going to the back door. What was he doing now?

Coming back into the kitchen, she didn't see Reno. She was about to ask her dad where he went but stopped herself. She didn't care. Or at least she shouldn't care. This was her not caring.

"Are you hungry, Mew-Maw?" She needed to take care of her family and not think about Reno.

It started working and then he walked back in. A wrapped plate in his hand. "We almost forgot the brownies. It's a lot of food. I hope it's okay that I called a friend of mine. I'm doing work in their kitchen. They could use a good homemade dinner so I went ahead and invited him and his wife over. I hope it's alright?"

Heat climbed up her neck. Was he serious? "I don't think—" Her father cut her off.

"Sure!" Mundo smiled. "The more the merrier. Looks as if your mother sent over enough to feed an army."

The frustration she was feeling just moved to borderline contempt. "You invited someone to come over, now?"

He held her gaze and grinned. "Yep. Should be here in about fifteen minutes. He happens to be a neighbor of sorts. You know him. Victor Villa."

She blinked. "Dr. Villa?"

"I think you're right. Yes. He is a doctor. Anyway, he's bringing his sweet wife too." He went to the stove and turned it on.

"She's a neurologist." Lyrissa took the top pan and opened it. All the anger was gone and just a hint of worry remained. She blinked a couple of times. He must have called Dr. Villa outside. He knew her grandmother would never agree to go in. "Thank you."

The urge to cry was ridiculous.

Edith harrumphed. "Well, I like Beverly and Victor, so if you're going to sneak in a doctor, they're good ones. Boy, get a couple of plates and set the table for them." Edith gave directions and stopped grumbling now that guests were coming.

Lyrissa grabbed a tortilla and gave him a pointed look. "After dinner, we're setting up a schedule to go over reading strategies."

His smile faded. "Okay. But don't get frustrated when you discover how pointless your mission is."

"If you come with an open mind don't be surprised if you find yourself doing things you didn't think you could do." It was her favorite part of her job.

She needed to be very careful, because she was starting to see him in a whole new light, and it wasn't good for her heart.

There was a knock at the door. She put her smile firmly in place. Time to entertain.

Chapter Eight

Lyrissa glanced at her watch. Her father and grandmother would soon be home from her doctor's appointment. Lyrissa had been on the phone longer than anticipated. But it was for a worthy cause. The boys would be enrolled and start school in the fall, and she had a summer job. Perfect for building her résumé. Her life was getting back on track.

While she was on the phone, Reno had arrived and took the boys to the barn. Stepping through the partially open door, she scanned the space for them. She squinted against the drastic lighting shift. She didn't see much, but it was too quiet. Where had they gone?

Today was the third round of lessons. The topic of her hospital visit never came up and she liked it that way. It was too awkward. He probably had no memory of it, and she was happy not telling him. There was no way he meant to ask her to marry him.

He was already embarrassed by his reading skills. She didn't want to make him feel worse.

The boys' favorite horses were still here so they hadn't gone riding. A giggle came from the far end of the barn, followed by someone shushing.

Placing each foot with care, she moved to the back of the barn. With a tilt to her head, she listened for any other sounds.

In the far-left corner, she saw the bottom of boots. All three of them were on their bellies halfway under a platform with hay. Bennett and Ray-Ray were on one side of the ladder that went to the loft and Reno was on the other side.

Not sure what was going on, she waited.

"I got one!" Bennett's excitement was clear.

"Be gentle." Reno's voice was low and soothing. "We don't want to hurt them."

Bennett scooted backward. Once he cleared the edge of the platform, he sat up. A black-and-white kitten was in his arms.

"Come here, kitty, kitty," Ray-Ray whispered. "I'll be a good friend."

"I think I can reach her," Reno said.

Bennett turned and saw her. His eyes filled with excitement for the first time since she met him. "We found kittens. Two. This one is black-and-white. The other's orange."

The kitten hissed and tried to get away. Bennett held on tight. Behind him, Reno handed Ray-Ray a small orange fluffball. It immediately snuggled closer to the little boy. "It likes me," he whispered to the purring kitten.

She had to smile. "I can hear purring from here. I think the black one wants to go back to its hiding place."

"She's just scared." He held out a piece of cheese and the kitten stilled then ate it. "She needs to learn she can trust me." He scratched her ears. "I'll put her back. Then she'll know I won't hurt her." He went back to the platform and hung out under there for a while.

"Can we keep them?" Ray-Ray was stroking his now-sleeping kitten.

This was not good. "Uhm. Cats belong in the barn. Dad strongly believes they have a job on the ranch, and they won't do it if they're pampered in the house."

Ray-Ray looked as if he was about to cry. Reno dropped to one knee in front of the little boy. "You should ask Mundo. He might say yes."

"Ask Mundo what?" Her father entered the barn.

Lyrissa jumped, hand over her heart. Reno laughed. "You look like you got caught doing something you're not supposed to do."

"Benny and I want to keep the kittens," Ray-Ray said, charging in without any tact.

Mundo frowned. "Nope. They belong in the barn. You can visit them. We'll need to catch them and the momma cat to take them in to the vet. Make sure they're healthy, and we don't get overrun with barn cats. But they do not ever come into the house. They're happier out here."

Ray-Ray hugged his closer.

Before more tears could fall, Reno stood. "What did the doctor say?"

With a snort, Mundo shook his head. "All the tests just proved she's healthier than most women ten years her junior. They said it was probably a vas—" He sighed. "I can't remember, but I wrote it down. It's caused by extreme emotional stress. The blood flow to the brain stops and you pass out. It's a way for the brain to reboot and get the blood flowing again. So, they advise she—" He glanced at the boys. "Well, I guess you can figure out what—or better yet, who—she should avoid."

"Daddy, I'm so sorry." She hugged her dad. Ray-Ray was watching them intently.

"Did Momma make Mew-Maw sick?" he asked.

Mundo walked over to him and put an arm around his shoulder. "Your Mew-Maw's temper made her sick. Yelling and screaming is not good for the body, mind or spirit. Do you want to go visit her? She went to tend her garden. Which means pulling weeds. She says it settles her."

"We should go help her." He smiled up at Mundo. "Bennett! Daddy wants us to go help Mew-Maw in her garden."

"Do I have to? I want my kitten to get used to me," Bennett yelled as he went back under the platform.

Ray-Ray hushed his brother. "Daddy says yelling is bad for you. But working in the garden and helping others makes you strong." He looked up at Mundo. "Right?"

"Couldn't have said it better myself," Mundo chuckled. "Bennett, get out from under there. We need to leave so these two can get on with their date."

"No! It's not a date," she protested. Heat climbed her neck. The thought of dating Reno was more exciting than it should be. Was she begging to have her heart broken?

She couldn't look at him. His smiling, charming face would be her downfall. He'd be all nice until he was bored, or something better came along. "Daddy, there is nothing between Reno and me."

The bullet-fast denial hurt his pride and his heart.

It also answered a question he had been tossing around in his head. The answer would be no if he asked her out. *Note to self. Don't ask her on a date.*

Of course, her answer would be no. She was trying to teach him how to read. Who wanted to go on a date with a guy who couldn't read the menu? He just always ordered the same or waited for others to order so he could copy them.

"We're friends." She looked at him, worry etched in her face. "Right?"

And he would do anything to make her happy, so he gave her his best smile and agreed. "No dating going on here."

"I'm just helping him with some of the chores around the ranch. I'm cheap labor. We're just friends, so don't get any ideas."

"Yep. Just friends." He would always be in the friend zone with Lyrissa.

Her shoulders relaxed and took a deep breath as if the weight of the world was lifted from her.

"Well, that's a shame." Mundo frowned.

Great. Reno made one person happy and upset the other. This was not a good day for him. They stood in silence as they watched Ray-Ray put his kitten back. Then the trio of Martinez males went to the big house to help Edith with the garden.

He didn't feel like doing a lesson today. He wanted to work in the garden too.

"I'm so sorry." Lyrissa broke into his thoughts.

"I should have let Dad think we were dating. It would be an easy way to explain all the time we're spending together. But I don't want to lie to him." She stuffed her hands in her jean pockets.

"No worries, teacher. Are we going out on horseback today or going to the beach?" He shifted and looked around. He still wasn't comfortable with her teaching him to decode the written language. It forced him to sit in the horrible, vulnerable place he hated. His whole life had been an exercise in covering it up. Now, he was exposed and raw.

"Today I have a few things I want to try that require sitting and some sort of table. I do want to stay outdoors. The front porch swing work for you?"

At the end of their first lesson, she had told him he was a kinesthetic learner. His body needed to be moving for maximum learning.

He had never heard the word before. But apparently, mixed with dyslexia, a traditional school setting was not a good fit.

It made sense. He had just thought he preferred outdoors and working with his hands. The lessons she did with him were more like games.

"Lead the way, teacher." He held the barn door open.

"Thank you for keeping an eye on the boys. You've really helped with their adjustment."

"They're good kids."

"I totally agree. Let's go through the kitchen so I can pick up my supplies."

Once settled into the swing, she introduced new strategies to see how he responded to those. About forty-five minutes into the lesson, he read a line without stumbling.

His eyes went wide, and he looked up at her. "It worked." He moved his finger along the rose-colored transparent filter and continued to read. He paused over one word and couldn't get it. With a grunt, he leaned back in the swing.

"Don't get frustrated. You've done great today."

He scoffed.

"You're an amazing man. Don't let this one thing define you." She gathered the papers and filters. "I think we should stop for the day. Brain work takes a lot of energy."

"You're the amazing one." He leaned forward without thinking. "The phone call earlier. Was it good news?"

She raised her head then froze. Their faces were less than six inches apart. If one of them leaned the slightest, they could be kissing. Five seconds. Five years. He had no sense of time or space. It was the two of them and she was not moving away.

Afraid she would bolt, he held perfectly still and waited.

She blinked but didn't move. "Uhm. The call? Yes. It was the school. They confirmed the boys' paperwork was complete for school next year and I got the part-time summer job with the special ed department." Her eyes moved but then came back to him. "It's perfect for my résumé."

Résumé. That's right. She was leaving. Did he just shift closer, or was it her? It was her. He was pretty sure he hadn't moved.

"You smell really good." Her eyes went wide. Jerking back, she slammed her lids shut. A guttural groan escaped passed tightly pressed lips. "Did I say that aloud? I didn't mean it. I mean, you do smell good. But I didn't mean to say it. Is it a new cologne or shampoo? Okay, I'm going to stop talking now."

He tucked a loose strand of hair behind her ear and gave her a lopsided grin. For the first time, he had hope. Maybe she would say yes. "We could go on a real date. No deep lifetime commitment. Just a fun date." He searched her face for any hint of agreement and held his breath. *Please say yes. Please.*

No would probably be the smarter answer for both of them. Once again, it was the wrong place and time. But his stupid heart wanted a *yes*. It wanted to spend real time with her.

If they didn't take a risk now, it would never

happen. She leaned toward him. He could feel
the echoes of her heartbeats. He could see a *yes*
hanging on the edge of her lips.

Chapter Nine

A car coming down the driveway broke the trance she had fallen into.

Whoa. She had been so close to…to kissing him? Saying *yes* to a date with Reno? Her heart raced as if she had just run a mile at a full-on sprint.

Shaking her head, she stood and turned to the car that had just parked in front of the house. People didn't just drive out to their place. The driver was talking to someone in the seat behind them. The back door opened.

Deeann Herff Martinez adjusted her large, floppy hat and sunglasses, then looked around before stepping away from the car. The car backed up and left the way it came.

Leaving the woman who gave birth to her standing alone in the drive.

No. She was not allowing that woman to create havoc. Rushing down the steps, she blocked Dee from stepping foot on the porch.

"Oh, my beautiful Lyrissa." Her mother came forward and went to hug her, but Lyrissa put her hand up and stepped back. "Don't come any closer."

A warm hand gently touched her back. Turning, she found Reno. He wasn't looking at her. He was staring down at her mom.

"Deeann, what are you doing here?" His always friendly voice was uncharacteristically stern.

Her clear, green eyes darted back between the two of them. "Who's this good-looking fellow? Do you have a sweetheart here in Port Del Mar?"

"No. You—"

"Baby girl. I know you're mad at me and you have every right to be." Dee batted her lashes as the tears built up. "I thought I was helping everyone. It was going to be grand for us all. But Harrison turned out to be a con artist and a bad influence. He had me making bad choices. You know I lose myself and make horrible decisions. I'm so sorry." She moved toward Lyrissa again, but Reno gently stepped between them. Not completely in front of her, but enough to hinder any attempt of Dee's to reach her.

Her mother made a pathetic whimpering sound. "I came home to beg your forgiveness. And to see my baby boys." Tears welled up in her big green eyes. "I *am* so sorry for the hurt I caused." She fisted her hands against her chest. "I know I messed up. This time I want to make it right."

Lyrissa put her hand in Reno's. He squeezed it, reassuring her that she wasn't alone. "Mom, you have to leave. You're not welcome here."

Her mother let the tears fall full force now. "Oh, baby girl. Please don't do this to your momma. I don't have anywhere to go. Harrison took all the money. He left me with nothing after I gave him everything. I trusted the wrong person."

The heat started at Lyrissa's chest. Did her mother even listen to herself? "I've trusted the wrong person too. But not again. You stole everything from me then abandoned your sons. You can't just walk back into our lives. Go find a way to start over somewhere else. Not here."

"What about my momma? What happened while I was on the phone with her? Mundo's not returning my calls. Is she okay?" Her chest moved with each heavy breath and panic filled her eyes. "He always answers my calls. What's wrong?"

Her father had stopped communicating with Dee? That was a first.

If her father didn't want to talk to Dee, then there was no way she'd allow her to stay on the ranch for a minute more. "She passed out because you upset her. That's what you do. You hurt people and I'm not going to allow you to hurt the people I love anymore. Leave, now."

"I'll take her to town." Reno stepped closer to Dee. "I'm Reno Espinoza. I'll take you to my mom's until you figure out where you're going next."

"No." It was a whimper. "This is my home—"

"You left us a long time ago." Lyrissa pushed down every bit of emotion and stared at the woman who had caused so much damage to her family. "Go get help. Professional help."

She hit her chest. "I'm still Gavin and Edith's daughter. I belong here as much as you do." She pointed at Lyrissa. "Your dad was just a ranch hand when I started dating him and...." She took a deep breath and patted her hand against her chest. "Sorry. You can't imagine how upsetting this all is."

Dee looked at Reno and smiled. "You were just a boy last time I saw you. I didn't even recognize you." Turning to Lyrissa, she nodded. "I'll go visit Mrs. Espinoza and text your dad. He'll come pick me up. He always does. I'm going to make this right, baby girl. I promise."

Lyrissa's stomach twisted and acid burned her throat. She didn't even bother to point out that promise had been made more times than she could count.

Reno put his hand on Dee's elbow. "That's my truck." He gently led her away.

Dee paused and looked back. Tears still soaked her fake lashes. "I'll be back for dinner. I love you."

Lyrissa held herself straight as Reno opened his passenger door. She would be gone before—

"Momma!" Ray-Ray came running around the corner of the house and flew past Lyrissa.

No.

He flung himself at his mother. Wrapping his arms around her, he buried his face in her stomach. "I told Benny you would come back."

Spinning around to see where he came from, she found different degrees of devastation on the faces of her father, Benny and Mew-Maw.

Reno froze. *This was not good.*

"Oh, Ray-Ray. Benny. I'm home. Come give some love to your momma." One arm went wide while she held Ray-Ray close to her. Bennett stood alone, not moving. His face, a hard mask. There was so much hurt and distrust radiating from the boy.

Mundo's jaw flexed. His eyes narrowed as if not sure what he was seeing. Edith was at his side. Her hand wrapped around his bicep. None of them moved forward.

"Mundo?" Dee's voice was smaller now. "I'm home."

The older man stood straight and shook his head. "This is not your home. Not anymore." He reached for Bennett and pulled him close. "What are you doing here?"

"I wanted to see my babies. Thank you for taking care of them. I—"

"You are not taking my sons anywhere. They're home and they'll stay here until they're old enough to decide for themselves."

Dee blinked as if not understanding. "But you said you'd always wait for me."

"That was before you stole from our daughter, abandoned our sons. The ones you've hidden from me. And before you pushed your mother to an unhealthy state. You are no longer welcome in my home."

Reno stepped forward. "I was about to take her to mom's."

Edith walked to the front of the truck. "She can stay in her old room in the main house. Until we can all calm down."

"Edith?" Mundo turned to his mother-in-law. "Are you sure you want to—"

"She's my daughter. She needs a place to rest." The older woman stood straighter. "This is temporary. No drinking or anything else. You will be up early with me and do whatever work needs done."

"Of course, Momma." Dee rubbed her sleeve under her nose. "Thank you."

"I'm doing this for your boys. And your daddy. Also, to make some of my wrongs right." She shook her head. Decades of regret filled her eyes and she looked older than she had in the morning.

Reno's jaw hurt from the tension. Lyrissa and her family didn't deserve this kind of drama. "Are you sure, Edith? My mom always has a room ready for anyone who needs it. To give you all some time." For what, he wasn't sure.

"No. She can stay with me. But one misstep and you're gone. If you do anything to hurt my family—" she pointed around her "—you'll be off this ranch forever."

Dee hugged Ray-Ray tighter. "I missed my boys. I missed all my family. Hitting rock bottom made me realize how much I love you. I'm so sorry."

"Actions speak louder than words, Deeann. So, show us. Come on." She walked to her daughter and picked up the one small travel bag. "Let's get you settled at the main house."

Dee held the hand of her youngest son, and paused as they passed Bennett. "Benny, will you come with me?"

He stepped closer to Mundo and wouldn't make eye contact with his mother. Mundo put an arm around his shoulder.

After a few long seconds of silence, she nodded and picked up Ray-Ray. "You have to tell me everything you've done on the ranch."

He nodded but stared at his older brother. Confusion was stamped all over his young face.

"It's okay, Ray-Ray," Bennett told his brother. "It's going to be alright."

A knot twisted Reno's heart over the older boy giving his brother permission to be with their mother despite his own pain. They stood in silence as they watch the trio go.

Mundo hugged the boy. "You are a good brother and you're right. All will be good. Is it okay if I take one of the horses out? I need to clear my head and spend time with God."

"Of course, Daddy." Lyrissa went to him and wrapped him in a tight hug. "I tried to get her to leave before y'all saw her. I'm so sorry."

"It's all good, cowgirl. We'll get through this. We're in God's hands. Bennett, do you want to go with me or stay?"

The boy's troubled gaze darted between his sister and father.

Reno tapped the hood of his truck. "I thought I'd take these two to my sisters' bakery. How does that sound?"

Sister and brother both nodded.

"That's a great idea. Your sisters' pastries make everything better." Mundo patted Reno's shoulder. "Thank you, son. You've been a blessing to my family."

"I've learned more from you than I had in all my years in school. Which might not be saying much, but it means a great deal to me. You're a good man, Mundo, and a great father."

Mundo grabbed him and pulled him in for a full-out hug, slapping him on the shoulder. "Thank you." With that, he turned and went back to the barns.

The air was heavy. Reno had a job. He had to bring back the smiles. "Y'all ready for the best sweets in the world? We need to get to town before they sell out of everything."

Should he tell a story or a joke? What did they need right now to deal with today's pain? He sighed. Today was an accumulation of years of broken promises and hurt. He was at a loss how to make it better.

Silence filled the cab of his truck as they passed the city limit sign.

Chapter Ten

There was a muffled sniff from the back seat. Bennett was trying to hide the fact he was crying. Lyrissa's heart was twisted with guilt and the unfairness of life.

"Bennett?" She turned around and reached over the seat. "Hey. That was a rough scene back there. It's okay if you're upset, angry, confused or all the above. This is a safe place—you can talk to us. You know you can tell me anything."

The silence hung heavy in the air as they gave him space to speak. He adjusted his position so he was looking at them instead of the passing landscape. "Is she going to make us leave?" His voice was low and shaky.

"Oh. No, sweetheart. I've got you enrolled in school. Dad is on both of your birth certificates as your father. Something we're all grateful for. This is your home. For as long as you want."

Reno nodded in agreement. "If she leaves, she can't make you go with her. She would have to go to court, and I don't see her doing that. And no judge would take you away from a stable home."

"Why did she come back now?" Bennett asked. "How can she show her face after what she did? Then pretend to love us. We shouldn't have left Ray-Ray with her."

"I don't think she pretends to love us. It's the addiction. It's loud and demands all her attention. It lies to her, and she turns around and repeats those lies as if they're truth. I wouldn't have left him alone with her either. He's with Mew-Maw. And Dad is on the ranch. She might be our mother, but we don't have to trust her."

"But she is our mom."

Reno tapped the top of the steering wheel and glanced in the rearview mirror. "She is. God has known from the very beginning. He won't let you go. You also have two great siblings you can count on. And a grandmother and father who will do whatever it takes to protect you."

He eased past a slower car whose occupants were sightseeing. "I lost my dad when I was very young, and your father filled that gap for me. Your mother might not be the kind of mother you need, but there are other women in your life who will fill that role. Women you can rely on to have your best interests at heart. Families are a mix of people we are related to and people who come into our lives as we need them, if we pay attention."

He was messing this up. Life was so much easier if he was just expected to make people smile. "Does any of that make sense?"

"No." Bennett huffed and flopped back against the seat.

He glanced at Lyrissa. Oh no. She had tears in her eyes. She didn't cry. What had he done? "I'm sorry."

"No, don't be." She smiled at him and waved at her face. "Ignore this." Not a huge, laughing smile, but a sincere, gentle curve of her lips. "You're right." She looked back at Bennett.

"I had other women who stepped in and guided me as any good mother would. First Mew-Maw. She's tough but she'll always be on your side. Trust her. I also had my best friend's mother. Reno's mother. Ms. Espinoza. She's the one I think of when I think what a mother should be. All of Reno's older sisters are outstanding role models. We can learn what not to do from our mother, but we can learn how to love from others. You'll get to meet a couple of his sisters today."

Reno parked in front of a colorful storefront on the corner of a strip. People filled the chairs and tables, which were arranged under a colorful awning. "They have so much love to give they had to open a bakery to let it flow over to the whole county."

He was right. His family was a cornerstone in the community. Her family, not so much.

Opening his door, he paused. Everything felt unresolved. They had allowed Bennett to talk about the reappearance of their mom, but Lyrissa hadn't really said anything. "We told Bennett this was a safe place to talk about what happened. It is for you too. I also know you hate coming into town. How are you doing?" He resisted the urge to reach out and hold her.

She chuckled. "I was so ready to get off the ranch I didn't even think about the people I might see in town. You know what? I'm not going to let the gossip and judgment stop me from doing something I want to do."

She reached across his cab and took his hand. "I forgot I had more friends than enemies in Port Del Mar. I allowed them to take up too much space in my brain. I'm looking forward to seeing your sisters again." Turning away from him, she studied the ocean across the street. Her throat worked as she visibly swallowed. "As for my mom? I'm so angry and scared. It's complicated and I'm not sure what to do."

She shook her head and looked at her brother. "When I saw her standing there, I just wanted to get her off the ranch before she could see any of you. I thought if I could keep her far away, I would be protecting you from getting hurt. I don't trust her. I don't think I ever will. But my dad, our dad, has forgiven her over and over. As much as I love him, I resent his forgiveness of her actions. I'm afraid to be like him or that I might be like her if I let myself have fun."

Now holding Bennett's hand, she squeezed it. "If you're confused and hurt, it's okay. So am I." She turned to Reno. "Thank you for offering to take her to your mother. I'm not sure if that would have been fair to your family, though."

"My family can handle anyone or anything."

"People are starting to stare. We should go in?"

"I'm hungry." Bennett took off his seat belt.

"Okay, get ready for lots of questions. They've noticed how much time I've spent at the ranch and have been sending out scouts to gather information. Since your visit to the hospital, they've turned up the heat. Bringing you here will be a total free-for-all." He put his hands on his steering wheel. "What was I thinking? This was a bad idea. Let's go somewhere else."

His sister Josefina opened the glass door and waved at them, then lifted her hands as if to ask what the holdup was.

Lyrissa laughed. A lightness began in her

chest she wouldn't have thought possible. "I think it's too late. If you drive away now, it will look so much worse. The whole pack will be after you. I don't think you could return home."

Bennett's eyes went wide. "How many sisters do you have? You can stay with us. We have an extra bed upstairs. You can have the big one."

"I might have to take you up on that. I have my mother, five sisters and a brother. All older. All but two live in town. Three of my siblings live on the same street as my mother."

"Do you still live with your mother?" Bennett sounded horrified.

"I live in an apartment over the garage."

Bennett raised his brows. Great, now he was being judged by an eight-year-old. "You know, it's not unusual in our family to live with multiple generations. My mom's getting older and—"

"It's okay. We're also multigenerational on the ranch." She looked at Bennett, chin down and her brows raised. "Come on, let's go. Reno is procrastinating."

"That is probably true," he agreed with a chuckle.

Josefina held the door open for them. "Come in. You're just in time, *mijo*. We need a man's opinion and now we have two. It's good to see you again, Lyrissa. This must be Bennett. Hi. I'm Josefina." She hugged Reno then Lyrissa.

"Can I hug you? We're huggers unless other-wise told." She grinned and opened her arms.

Bennett dropped his chin but stepped into her hug.

"Follow me." The whimsical seating area was a mix of fairy-tale tea party and traditional Mexican flare. Two of his nieces were behind the counter. They waved and came around to hug him and greet his guests. "So, Tio Bridges is turning an eye away from child labor laws."

Nica, Josefina's daughter, rolled her eyes, but had a big grin on her face. "We tried that, but a family-owned business doesn't count."

His sister swatted at him. "Stop that. The girls are hardly here part-time. With Resa's wedding, we're shorthanded." She went through the back doors. "All hands on deck. You're coming, aren't you?" She glanced at Lyrissa as she held the swinging door open.

They stepped into a dreamland of pies and fancy cakes. Reno had grown up with his sisters' baking brilliance, but this was on a whole new level. "Has Resa or Enzo seen this?" They were the happy couple getting married next weekend. They were both low-key when it came to events and parties.

Margarita, his oldest sister, popped up from behind the sweet monstrosity. "*Mijo!* We're having a difference of opinions about the groom's cake and pie bar."

"Pie bar?" His gaze went over the twenty different pies sitting on a menagerie of pedestals.

"We are also having a lively debate about the wedding cake." Josefina moved to the side of the table that held four different wedding cake tops. From glass swans to a cowboy couple, each a different style.

"No. We are not discussing the cake. I have decided and it's done."

"You cannot make a seven-layered cake with a carrot cake–cream cheese mix."

"I can and I will." They kept arguing.

He mouthed *sorry* to Lyrissa and Bennett.

She giggled.

He cleared his throat to get their attention. And he had been worried they were going to grill him. "I don't understand," he said carefully. "Shouldn't Resa and Enzo be the ones to decide?"

Margarita threw her hands up and rolled her eyes. "You would think so. But she says she just wants a simple cake. She also wants a carrot cake and cheesecake. She says that as if that is a thing. Do you know how hard it is to make a carrot cheesecake that has the right level of moisture? To top it off, it must feed three hundred people." She rubbed her head.

"That is why I say we just make the top for her and the rest one of our nice traditional flavors."

"Have you tasted my carrot cheesecake?" She cut a big slice, grabbed three spoons then marched over to him, Lyrissa and Bennett. "Here." She handed them each a utensil. "Try this."

They all did as were told. His eyes went wide. He was used to the wonders his sisters created but this was… He swallowed. "This might be the best thing I've ever eaten."

Bennett nodded as he went back for a second scoop.

"I agree. I would have never imagined putting a carrot cake and a cheesecake together. This is…incredible." Lyrissa took another spoonful.

Margarita looked angry. He wanted more cake, but he stepped back.

"See." His oldest sister waved her hand around. "If I make just the top with this a few people will get it. Then we have three hundred other people upset because they hear about this cake, but I didn't make enough for everyone. That is not something I would do."

The sisters were in the middle of a staring contest. Risking their wrath, he stepped between them. "You're both right. Have you talked to Mom?"

In unison, they sagged. "No," his sisters said at the same time. "She already has too much on her plate, so we said we had this covered."

"I agree that when people come to an event

hosted by the Espinoza family, they know they are going to be fed well. It's more complicated, but what about a small traditional cake then cupcakes instead of a traditional seven-layer cake?"

"Oh. We can use fancy tulip liners and make them look like flowers. That's a great idea." Margarita rubbed her hands together. "We'll have to get a couple of stands. Wood painted white, four tiers."

"That'll work." Josefina nodded. "We would need less pies." She looked at Reno and Bennett. "Enzo is also not much help. He says he prefers pies to cake. I ask which pies. He says all. I try to corner him. Pecan? He says yes. Apple? Again, he says yes. Cherry? Chocolate? Yes and yes. You know what he said next?" She looked at them like they were the ones causing problems. Trying to be agreeable, they shook their heads. Reno would laugh aloud if it wouldn't upset his sister more than she already was.

"He says he also likes chocolate peanut butter pie, key lime, coconut cream, banana cream, strawberry and lemon meringue. Then he nodded his head and said 'I like all those.' He tells me to pick the one I want to make, and he'll be happy. What am I supposed to do with that?"

"So, we decided to make a pie bar. We were going to do ten, but I think with the cupcakes we should cut it back to five or three. Enzo is not going to be able to eat all of them anyway."

"Will you sample the pies and vote on the ones you think will make Enzo happy?"

With a hand on Bennett's shoulder, he tried to get his most serious face on. "It sounds like a tough job. But we've got this."

Bennett grinned. "I like your family's problems."

He laughed and he looked up at Lyrissa. She was smiling but it looked sad. He'd do anything to make her happy. But that wasn't his job. He focused on the pies.

His sisters were talking about the wedding to Lyrissa, but he didn't understand half of it. After a sample of each pie, he talked over the pros and cons of each slice with Bennett. It was serious stuff.

Margarita handed him a notebook and pencil. "Just write down the ones you like in order." She paused. "Oh. I'm sorry. I didn't… Do you…"

"It's fine. I'm good. Bennett and I got this. I know my numbers." He winked at her. Ever since they found out his secret, they had started acting like he was a helpless kid all over again.

"He's been doing great." Lyrissa filled the awkward silence.

"Oh, I'm sure he has. He is obviously super smart to be able to hide it so long from us. But

I'm sure that's not the only reason you've been spending so much time at the Herff Ranch."

And there it was. "I've been working as a part-time ranch hand. There's a lot of work that needs to be done."

Josefina joined them. A sly grin on her face. "Could be that we'll have another wedding to plan soon? You laid it on pretty thick in the hospital, baby brother." She wiggled her brows.

"Stop. You look ridiculous. You're a mother." He wouldn't allow his sisters to embarrass Lyrissa. "Just because you're taking credit for Resa and Enzo doesn't make you matchmakers."

His oldest sister leaned a hip on the worn farm table and looked at Lyrissa. "You know he always had a thing for you, but under all that charm and swagger he's pretty shy."

He rolled his eyes. "That's enough. We came to pick up some sweets for the house. Their mom is back on the ranch, and we came to town to get the best pastries around. A few empanadas and cookies. We don't need unsolicited advice."

She opened her mouth, but before she could get any words out Nica came through the swinging doors. "Mom. We're out of pecan pie in the front, and someone wants a slice. Do we have any more?"

"Yes. I'll bring it out." She picked up a pie and headed for the door. "So much to do and not enough time to get it all done." She paused with her back to the door. "Maggie, we'd be smart to have someone who's not family watch over the pie table." She pushed through the door.

"Josie does have a good idea every now and then." As far as he knew, they were the only ones ever allowed to call each other by those nicknames. His sisters were great people, but they exhausted him.

"We just came by for the goods. Are there any empanadas left?"

"No. We ran out about an hour ago. I have a pumpkin and strawberry already mixed for the morning. I could throw some together if you can wait."

"Oh, please don't do that." Lyrissa shook her head. "You have so many other wonderful treats. We'll save the empanadas for another day."

"Okay." She reached over and squeezed Lyrissa's hand. "Is everything okay? Is your mom in a good place?"

His heart slammed against his chest. This was the reason she hated coming to town. His sister had only good intentions, but still.

"We don't know yet." She nodded to Bennett. "We came into town to give her space to settle and for us to…be okay with it. She's staying with Mew-Maw in the main house."

"That's good. If there is anything we can do to

help, let us know. You spent so much time with Savannah growing up, you're an honorary Espinoza." She leaned in with a smirk. "And another Espinoza might have a crush on you."

"Will you stop?" He had known this was a bad idea. "You do realize that you make people extremely uncomfortable?" He couldn't believe that his sister was actually saying these things aloud.

"Oh, hush you. You would help her in a heartbeat."

"I would, but you're making more out of it than you should. You think you're being clever or cute. Well, you're not." He shoved his hands in his pockets.

Lyrissa patted his arm. "It's okay. She's just being a big sister. I always wanted one."

"Well, now you have two. Be careful what you wish for." Margarita laughed at her own joke. "There is something you can do for us." She held her hands up. "Feel free to say no, but we do need someone to keep an eye on the dessert table during the reception. Restock if needed. You wouldn't have to stand there all night. There might be someone who wants to get you on the dance floor. If you say yes, well, we would all be thrilled."

"Yes. To helping with the pies and cakes. No to dancing."

"What? You wouldn't want to dance with me?" He cleared his throat. That sounded way too high-pitched.

"That's not what I meant," she stammered.

He laughed. "Sorry." They needed to leave. His sisters had him acting like a child.

Lyrissa swatted him. "Now who's making this weird and awkward. Let's check to see what we can take with us."

He was coming to realize that dating Lyrissa would be a lifelong wish come true, but one look at her unamused face told him it was never going to happen.

"Y'all are both weird." Bennett grinned at Reno. "You should just date and make everyone happy. And I vote for the chocolate peanut butter pie. That would make me very happy."

If he had his way, he'd want to make the whole Martinez clan happy. They deserved it. But like so many of his other wishes and desires, it was beyond his capabilities.

Chapter Eleven

Lyrissa's room was full of light as she swayed side to side. In the mirror, the skirt swirled around her. She didn't wear dresses often and it made her feel pretty. She had been at Resa's bachelorette party when she confessed to Josefina that she didn't have anything to wear to the wedding. Which immediately prompted everyone to move from the kitchen where they were wrapping mason jars with ribbons to Josefina's closet, where they made her try on several dresses.

She almost teared up at the memory. It wasn't just Reno's sisters. She had been surrounded by cousins, coworkers and friends. She had never felt like she belonged anywhere. Until now. The place she ran from. Why was it so different this time?

Reno was right. She had been the one to keep people out. Last weekend, they pulled her in and didn't let go. Tears burned in her eyes. *Nope. Not getting emotional or attached. Refocus.*

Holding the soft material, she swirled again. The bold floral print of pinks, yellows and greens was not anything she would have ever tried on.

"Oh, baby girl. You're beautiful." Her mother came up behind her, laying her hand on Lyrissa's shoulder as they made eye contact in the mirror. "You're the best of your father and me."

Stuffing back a sigh, she smiled at the woman who had given her life and her biggest heartbreaks. "Thanks. You look nice too."

Every time they talked, her mother cried. At first, she saw it as manipulation. Now she wasn't so sure. Her mother seemed to be really trying and not pushing herself into the family.

There was so much pain, but she couldn't let her mother's unresolved issues ruin her family's life. She went to her dresser on the other side of the room and pretended to get something.

Dee sat in the chair at her desk. "I hear you and Mom are going early to help set up. That's very nice of you." She plucked at something on her skirt. "Your dad is taking me. I was thinking of not going, but Mundo loves to dance. I promised your dad I wouldn't drink. I promise it to you too."

"Don't worry about making promises, Mom. Just do the right thing. I'm not worried about others. I've decided that people not in my circle won't be allowed to keep me from being happy with the people I love."

"What? Everyone loves you. Just like they love your father. There are so many gossips in Port Del Mar, and they don't want me to be happy." Tears threatened to fall again. "Your dad is talking to me again and that's all that matters. I don't want to mess it up." She smoothed her skirt. "I have something to give you."

Without another word, she disappeared. On her way out, she passed Mew-Maw.

"What was she doing?" her grandmother asked.

"I'm not sure. She said she has something to give me." Lyrissa didn't have a good feeling. "Any ideas what it might be?"

"With that girl, I have no idea." Her grandmother was wearing a denim skirt with a white blouse, tall boots and lots of turquoise jewelry.

Dee came in with a box. She held it out to Lyrissa. "When I saw these, I hid them so Harrison couldn't pawn them too." Tears were falling. "I'm so sorry. If you never forgive me, I understand."

Taking the box, she lifted the lid. It was her great grandmother's necklace and wedding ring. It had more sentimental value than monetary. She thought they were lost forever. What was she supposed to say to her mother? Thanks for returning something she stole?

"I know you didn't trust me with them, Mom, but see? I took care of them." The silence was heavier than the elephant sitting in the middle of the room.

A knock on her doorframe saved her from spilling the heated words that were boiling under the surface. A very dashing Reno stood there, in a tux.

"I'm sorry. Do I need to come back?" He hesitated. "Or should I remind you that we need to leave now?"

She put the box on her dresser and grabbed her clutch. "We need to leave. They'll be waiting and you have pictures to be in." Without making eye contact, she rushed past her mother.

"Lyrissa?" Dee's voice carried all the hurt of someone who's been betrayed. How did her mother always manage to see herself as the victim?

"Not now, Dee." It was petty, but she knew it hurt her mother when she called her by her name. She kept moving forward and headed straight to Reno's truck.

On the porch, she stopped. His truck wasn't there. The door opened behind her. She turned. "Where's your truck?"

"I thought we would look too good to be in

that old work truck, so I borrowed Mom's SUV. She's with Margarita and didn't need it." He shrugged.

Mew-Maw stepped out behind him, laughing. "You borrowed your mom's car to take your girl to a dance. Does that make me the chaperone?"

Lyrissa glared at her grandmother. "Stop it. Reno and I are just friends. Why is everyone giving us a tough time about that?"

"Maybe because we all see something you're denying." Mew-Maw winked at Reno as if they were in on a joke together.

He opened the back door and helped Mew-Maw in the vehicle. "I'd say it's more likely that we're your chaperones. Someone needs to keep you out of trouble."

"Oh, I could use a bit of trouble. Keeps one young." She climbed in and clicked her seat belt.

Reno moved to the front passenger door. "Your carriage awaits, my lady." He bowed. "You look beautiful, by the way."

Heat climbed up her neck. "Thank you. You look rather dashing yourself."

They all settled in, sitting in silence as he drove the SUV off the ranch.

"Everything okay?" Reno asked.

"Sweetheart." Her grandmother's voice was uncharacteristically soft. "It's okay to be mad. She had no right to take a thing from you. But then to present Granner's jewelry as if it were a gift?" She clicked her tongue.

If she attempted to talk, she would cry. *Please Lord, remove this bitterness from my heart.*

"Is that what happened before I interrupted?" Reno glanced at her. The concern in his eyes was her undoing.

She nodded. "I don't understand why or how she is the person she is." She looked back at her grandmother. "You've been a solid rock for me. Daddy has always been there for me and for her. He never calls names or is harsh in any way. What happened to her? It scares me. She's my mother. What if…" Some fears were just buried too deep to unearth. "What happened to make her this way? I want to understand."

Her grandmother leaned forward and patted her shoulder. "She was such a sweet child, but stubborn. A true daddy's girl. We always butted heads. When I complained about her attitude, Gavin would laugh. He said we were too much alike."

"But I've never seen you drink, and you would never steal from anyone, especially your family or the church. She didn't learn it from you."

Her grandmother stared at the passing landscape. "When Gavin was killed in the accident, I lost my partner. My best friend. *My rock.* We lost the person who kept us balanced."

Her gaze went to her hands where she was twisting her wedding band. "I'm old-school, you know. Raised by a Texas rancher who was raised by a Texas rancher. This land can be harsh, and you got to be tough to build a home here."

"But you've never given me anything but love and support." Lyrissa reached out her hand. The work-worn, leathered skin of her grandmother grasped her in return.

"I'm happy to hear you say that. But I didn't react to his death with the grace that Reno's mother did at the loss of her husband."

"My mother had my older sisters and Bridges. A lot of the burden fell on his shoulders to keep the family together." His gaze shifted to the rear-view mirror for a moment, then went back to the road. "I was too young to understand or appreciate it at the time, but it might be the reason I learned to hide any problems I had. I didn't want to upset anyone. If they were happy, then my world was safe."

Her heart twisted at the thought of a small Reno who believed his value was making others smile. She longed to hold his hand, but nope. No. She turned to her grandmother.

"Mew-Maw. This is not your fault."

"I gave her three days to cry." She tapped her chest three times. "That's what I said. Three days. Then we had a ranch to run. Life didn't take a break for death. She was fifteen and I denied her time to feel her grief."

"Oh Mew-Maw. You denied yourself too."

Her grandmother nodded. "Yes. When you came home this time with my grandbabies that I didn't even know about?" She shook her head. "I broke. I couldn't take it. I went to Pastor Rodriguez for help."

"Really? You always said—"

"Posh." She waved her silver-and-turquoise-covered hand at Lyrissa. "I repeated what my grannie and daddy told me. And it is a bunch of hogwash. Look at Reno and his family. They've suffered tragic losses and tough times. I wanted to know how they did it. Pastor Rod has been immensely helpful. One of the first things he gave me was this little book on the seven stages of grief. Do you know anything about it?"

"I do. And it's not only a process we need to get through the death of a loved one, but any major loss." She sat back. The epiphany of her own grief swamped her mind. Her mother wasn't dead, but somewhere in her early childhood she had lost the mother she had loved and trusted.

Some of the anger dissipated. It was okay to grieve the mother she had lost. It was okay not to trust Dee or expect any motherly reactions from her. She had her brothers, her father and

Mew-Maw. They were her family and loved her as much as she loved them.

Reno nodded. "You're going to come through this and be stronger. So will the boys with family support."

"And counseling," Lyrissa said, agreeing. Determination replaced anger. "I'm grateful she brought them home. I am not going to let her take them away. Even if it means I have to stay in Port Del Mar."

"Oh, you don't need to worry about the boys," Mew-Maw said with a reassuring firmness. "Your father has that under control. He has a lawyer drawing up paperwork. She isn't getting a free pass from him any longer."

"Really? Why hasn't he talked to me about this? I was surprised when Dad didn't let her move in with him." Lyrissa shook her head then grinned at her. "It was a total role reversal. It was the first time I saw him stand up to her and tell her no. That gives me hope more than anything else."

"Holding her accountable is the only way she has a chance of getting better. Your dad sees that now." Mew-Maw flopped back against the seat. "If I hadn't been so hard on her after the death of Gavin, I might have a different daughter."

"Or not," Reno said. "Never seen redoing the past done successfully, even in fiction." He grinned. "But you have today. You have God, and you have each other. That's one life lesson my mom made sure each of her kids understood. *Mi familia.*"

"And tonight is about celebrating that." Warmth snuggled in around her. And for the first time since stepping back into Port Del Mar, gratitude hummed in her heart.

Mew-Maw snapped her fingers in the air. "Dancing. You're saving one for me. And my beautiful granddaughter." She clapped with childish joy.

Shaking her head, she looked at Reno. She knew without a mirror that her cheeks were red. "You don't have to dance with me. I have two left feet."

He winked. "So, we'll only turn to the right. You owe me a night of dancing." He whispered it low and soft as if making a promise...or a threat.

Reno parked the SUV by the back door of the bakery. It didn't take long to load up the pies and cupcakes. The aroma made her mouth water. Reno looked at her with a knowing gaze. "I don't think they will miss one or two."

She put her hand up. "Don't you dare tempt me. You're a bad influence, Reno Espinoza."

"I'm good at everything I do." He winked and she groaned.

Mew-Maw laughed. "Come on, you two. Stop flirting and let's get the pies set up."

Reno joked around with Mew-Maw. Once they arrived at the Painted Dolphin, she found Elijah, the owner. He directed them to the tables set up for the desserts.

Josefina was putting the last touches on the wedding cake. "Remind me to never again insist on making the cake for a wedding when I'm also a bridesmaid. I'm too old for this."

She placed the last tiny sugar flower on the side of the round top cake. It was exquisite.

"You'll forget by the time the next wedding comes around," Reno told her.

"You're the only one left, baby brother. So, I guess I don't have to worry about it."

"What? You're my first choice for best man. Or do you think I'm not getting married?" He took the spoon out of the extra icing and licked it. "Hey Lyrissa, want to lick the spoon with me?"

Josefina took the spoon from him. "I'm going to hit you over the head with this if you don't behave. So sorry Lyrissa that you got put on baby-sitting duty for my brother."

"What?" Reno pressed his hand to his heart in an overly dramatic move. "No. You got it wrong. I'm on bodyguard duty."

The DJ was setting up and doing sound checks.

"This is a great song. Dance with me." He held his hand out to Lyrissa.

She glared at him. "Don't you have prewedding duties too? What time are you supposed to be there?"

He shrugged and pointed to his sister. "I figure when she leaves, I leave."

Josefina was arranging the cake top over the tower of flower-looking cupcakes. From there, she joined Mew-Maw and helped her with the tea, lemonade and water station.

"Come on. One dance?" He gave Lyrissa his big, puppy dog face with that bottom lip sticking out.

Shaking her head, she put the last pie on a short pedestal. It really was pretty with all the spring flowers in mason jars and yellow ribbons. "Why am I surrounded by people who don't take life seriously?"

He looked hurt. Closing her eyes, she took a deep breath. "Sorry. I'm just on edge with Mom and—" She looked at the dessert table. "Your sisters are amazing, and they trusted me to set this up. Please let me focus. Find something useful to do."

With a sigh, he put his hands in the pockets of his black pants.

His sister walked by. "See? I told you he needed a babysitter."

"You people are way too uptight for your own good. When you get the chance to laugh, do it. Laughter is always an excellent choice." The smile was back on his face, and he started dancing in place.

"I'll dance with you, cowboy." Her grandmother put her hand out.

"Mew-Maw, don't encourage him."

He winked at her as he spun her grandmother into a Texas Two-Step. When the song ended, he took his sister's hand and made her dance with him. She was laughing.

Her grandmother joined her. Gripping her shoulders, she laid her head against Lyrissa's for a brief second. "It's okay to have fun. He's right, you know. Laughter is a good choice, and you need more of it. Don't let your mother take the joy out of life. Reno wants to see you smile. He's a good man. You should give him a chance. I've seen how he looks at you and how hard he works to make you smile."

Past the dance floor, the horizon was endless where the ocean met the sky. "I'm kind of tired of people who just want to have a good time."

"Oh, sweet baby. My heart aches to see you happy."

She made sure to give her grandmother a big cheesy grin. "I know you mean well, but I have a bucketful of worries before I even think about dating."

"I spent my whole life working hard and not making time to laugh or cry. I lost my best friend and then my daughter in the process. Don't miss the opportunity to find joy because you're caught up in the past or worried about the future."

Lyrissa pulled the container full of glass pie covers out from under the table. "Right now, our job is to cover the pies so we can go to the wedding." And she prayed her mother didn't have too much of a good time. This would be her first social event in Port Del Mar in years.

"I just don't want Mom to embarrass the family. The Espinozas are such good people."

Laughter floated from the dance floor. Reno spun his sister around several times. Her head was back as she laughed.

Her grandmother nodded. "Your father and I will have your mom. If something happens, hopefully we can de-escalate before anyone notices. Make sure you enjoy yourself." They stood side by side and watched Reno with his sister. "There's nothing wrong with having fun. Your mom just uses it to hide. Reno's not like that. His love for life is real. Give him a chance."

Josefina swatted at her brother's chest and stepped back. She looked over at them. "Are y'all all set?"

"Yes," her grandmother answered. "It's going to be a beautiful night."

Reno looked straight at Lyrissa. "It's already more beautiful than I imagined."

Words like that would lead her heart to cave. It would only end in heartbreak. There wouldn't be any happy endings for her in Port Del Mar.

"Do you have Mew-Maw?" she asked him. "I'm going with Josefina to the wedding so I can help with all the children. They have a small herd to get down the aisle."

She ignored the disappointed look that flashed in his eyes. She smiled and pushed on, not giving him time to say anything to change her mind. "I'll see you there." She followed his sister to the parking lot.

Reno loved seeing his family happy. Resa's wedding had been as special as she was. Weddings and babies brought out the best in all his siblings.

He missed his sister Savannah, but he knew in his gut she had done the right thing by leaving with her husband. If it wasn't for Lyrissa, he'd feel very alone.

But she was leaving too. By the end of summer, she would be moving on to make a life somewhere else.

One of his nieces asked him to dance. No way

would he ever say no to his siblings' children. He had to enjoy them; he wouldn't be having any of his own anytime soon...or possibly ever. That soured his good mood. This was not a time for those ugly thoughts.

It was a popular opinion he was too much of a kid to want to settle down. It was a false opinion, but he wasn't doing anything to prove them wrong.

"*Tio*, I want a wedding just like Tia Resa's," the eight-year-old said as he led her around the dance floor.

Enzo's family ranch had been covered in fairy lights. They led to the barn where his sister and Enzo Flores promised to stand by each other for the rest of their lives. And it wasn't one of those trendy fake barns. The working barn still had a couple of horses in the stalls.

Now the party had moved into town at the Painted Dolphin, with a dance floor on the large deck looking over the water.

"It was beautiful," he agreed. She went on in more detail. He scanned the area for Lyrissa. He spotted her grandmother.

Mew-Maw had taken the opportunity to make a deal with Enzo's father about borrowing one of their bulls. Reno had to grin. That woman would use her last breath to make the ranch better.

The Painted Dolphin was on the most popular

pier in town. They even had a pirate ship docked right next to the large deck of the restaurant. The ship was set up for the kids to play. Bennett and Ray-Ray were both over there, having fun. Bennett had become fast friends with his brother's oldest son.

On Monday, he would be going to summer camp with his nephew. Cooper had invited Bennett to go home with Bridges and his wife tonight. It felt good to see the boys settle in and make connections in the community. He was proud that they were fitting in with his family.

The song ended and his niece ran off to join her cousins. He scanned the area for Lyrissa again. They were going to dance tonight, and she was going to smile. If he did his job right, he might even get to hear her laugh.

She didn't have to tell him how worried she was about her mother coming tonight. Her family was so focused on the unpredictable Dee, Lyrissa was often forgotten and left on her own.

Not that she asked him to worry about her. She made it clear that the friend zone had very strong barricades that he would not be crossing.

There she was. His heart lightened and his smile widened. She had returned to the pie table. Handing a plate to someone, she smiled, but it was her polite I'm-a-good-person smile. Not the one that made her eyes sparkle.

As he approached, she pulled a fresh pie from a cooler hidden under the table and removed the empty dish. She looked up and smiled. The same smile she had given the other person. That wouldn't do.

"The boys are having a great time in the pirate ship," he said as a greeting. She worried about them.

Her smile softened as she glanced over to where the ship was docked. The lights strung up the mast were reflected in the water. "That makes me happy. It looks straight out of a storybook. I'm so proud of the De La Rosas. Who would have ever guessed they would own half the businesses in Port Del Mar?"

"Hard work and dedication pays off. They're well respected. It didn't come easy, but they deserve it."

"It also took lots of faith." Elijah De La Rosa joined them. He picked up a plate with a piece of pecan pie and started eating. "God can work wonders when we open our lives to him. Your parents look happy tonight."

She laughed. It was a bit stiff, but he didn't think Elijah noticed. "Not something I would have ever predicted. But the night is still young. She has plenty of time to create a scene."

Elijah turned and scanned the dance floor. "The blessing and curse of a small town. Everyone knows you and everyone *knows* you. Can't hide the skeletons in the closet. Not when they want to come out and play. But like I said, with God anything and everything is possible. I'm a primary witness to that. If you need anything, let me know."

"Thank you."

He took the last bite of pie and nodded. "Have you checked out my pirate ship? It's really cool."

She laughed, a real laugh and Reno marked it in the win column. It was for Elijah but that didn't matter as long as someone reminded her to find joy in the day. Elijah moved to talk to another table. He was always playing host, making sure all was good.

"Come on. Dance with me." Reno held his hand out. "You've owed me since homecoming. And you've been watching your parents all night. You can get a closer look if we are on the dance floor."

She looked at the pies.

"No." He cut off any excuses her brain was forming. "I heard Josefina say that you just needed to keep an eye on the table to restock." He waved his hand over the delicious-looking table. His sisters did know how to feed people. "You just did that. So, unless you want me to get my sisters and tell them you are not having a good time, you better join me."

"Snitch." She tilted her head, hands on her hips. "Are you really blackmailing me with the threat of your sisters to get what you want?"

"Yep." He gave her his most charming grin. He held out his hand. "They can be a deadly force when their baby brother calls on them. But I don't need to ring the alarm, do I?"

With a shake of her head and a lopsided grin, she came around the table with her hand out. "Lead the way, cowboy."

Second point in the win column. He'd take it. He'd never felt lighter or prouder as he led her around the dance floor. As they moved with the other dancers, he didn't see anyone but her. They were on the third dance when she pulled him back to reality.

"Have you seen my parents?" She was looking over his shoulder, then hers. "They were out here the last dance. I don't see them at any of the tables either."

"It's okay, Lyrissa. Your dad has her. Everyone is having fun. The stars are over us. The moon is full and round. The breeze is cool. It's a perfect night. Relax and enjoy." He spun her away from him then pulled her back. With her head back she laughed. Score three for him.

Her sigh was so heavy it vibrated up his arms. It seemed like a happy sigh. He gave himself another point. As the song ended the DJ called all married couples to the floor. He moved Lyrissa to the side. Most of his siblings gathered and started dancing.

His mother, a widow for most of his life, smiled. "It's good to see my babies settled and happy." She hooked her arm through his. "You're next."

"Mom." He would love to be half of a happily married couple, but he didn't see it happening anytime soon. The wedding coordinator came over and asked for his mother's help with something. The younger couples left the dance floor as the number reached fifteen years.

How would it feel to be part of a couple that faced the day together every morning?

Josefina joined them. Eight years ago, she had returned home from college with a newborn. No husband and he had never asked. She looked out at the couples with longing.

"Hey sis. You okay?" He hated it when anyone he loved looked sad.

"Yea," she sighed.

He didn't buy it for a minute.

He nudged her. "The other day at a men's retreat, old Jose was asked how he'd managed to stay happily married for almost fifty years. You know what he said?"

She eyed him with suspicion and remained silent. Lyrissa leaned forward. "What did he say?"

Josefina shook her head. "Don't take the bait."

There were even fewer couples now that the number had reached thirty years.

"He told the young husbands, 'I treat her nice. Never went to bed angry. I spent some money on her. Best of all, I took her to Paris for our twenty-fifth wedding anniversary.' The men wanted to know what he had planned for their fiftieth wedding anniversary coming up. He proudly replied…" Reno paused, dragging out the suspense.

Josefina jabbed him with her elbow. "Get it over with."

"He said, 'I'm going to pick her up.'"

Bridges, who had come off the dance floor with his wife, laughed.

"That wasn't funny," his wife and Josefina said at the same time.

His brother grinned at him. "Come on. It was a little funny."

His sister snorted. "I got more important things to do than stand here listening to your dumb jokes."

"*Clever*. The word you were looking for *is clever*," he yelled after her as she walked away. But she was smiling, so he had done his job.

"I see what you were doing." Her eyes were worry-free as she looked up at him.

He leaned back to get a better look at her. "And what was that?"

"It's okay to let people be sad sometimes. It

might be what we need to get over whatever is running through our hearts. But out of love for your family, you have appointed yourself court jester and if you see someone slipping away from happy, you try to reset their course." She lifted her chin as if to dare him to dispute that.

"No comment." He loved that she really saw him, even in a way his family didn't, but it was also uncomfortable. "How about pie? I never got a piece, and you are queen of sweets tonight."

At the table, he picked up his favorite, pecan pie, and she was digging into a piece of key lime when Elijah came over. "Hey, would y'all step over here for a minute? I need to talk to you."

Reno's good mood evaporated at the other man's expression. Elijah was always a great host with an easy smile. This was something serious. Something they weren't going to be happy about. At least he was here to support her.

Chapter Twelve

As soon as they were out of earshot, Elijah took a deep breath. "Your mom got upset when someone asked him to dance. There was a little heated discussion. Your dad didn't want it to turn into a scene, so he took her home. Edith picked up the little one. They said the older boy was going home with Bridges's family. Everything is fine and Mundo wanted to make sure you didn't worry."

Any fun she was having was gone. He could see it in the droop of her shoulders.

"Thanks for giving us the message." Reno offered his hand, and they shook.

"No problem." He put a hand on Lyrissa's shoulder. "You know I've been there myself on both sides. If you need anything, let me know. I can connect you to resources. Even if she won't get help, the family needs support."

She nodded. "Thank you."

Once they were alone, he took her hand. "Do you want to go home? I can take you."

"No." Her gaze went past him, at the party going on under the star-filled sky. "I knew this would happen. I hoped it wouldn't, but she hasn't really changed."

"Don't let this ruin a great night. Your father and grandmother handled it."

Her glare came back to him, hot and hard. "They shouldn't have to handle her." She spun around and crossed her arms around her middle. "I want to be done, but I can't leave them. She needs to go to rehab, but she won't."

"Life's not fair and I'm so sorry you have to deal with this." Staying calm on the outside, he was frantically orchestrating a plan of distraction. "You said you missed the beach. The waves soothe you?"

He held out his hand and waited for her to take it for the second time that night. "It's a beautiful night for a walk on the beach. We can talk. I can tell you jokes."

She quickly shot that down with one hard glare.

He shrugged, not offended. "Or you can be sad. We can be silent, focusing on the texture of the sand and sound of the water. Maybe be still and listen for God's wisdom."

"Just about the time I think you are truly superficial, you throw in a curveball." She looked over his shoulder to the water behind him. "The beach does sound nice."

He took her around the edge of the party and down the pier. They were on the steps to the beach when Bennett found them.

"Is it true?" he asked. "Some woman flirted with Dad and Mom got mad. She got loud which means she was drinking, right? She promised not to drink. Why did you let her drink?"

"Bennett. I don't know what happened other than Dad took her home before there were serious problems."

"Mew-Maw picked up Ray-Ray and didn't say anything to me. They didn't tell me they were leaving. I need to get home. Ray-Ray needs me. I've always taken care of him when she gets like this. He'll be scared without me."

This was one of the reasons Lyrissa and he orchestrated the weeklong camp with Cooper. Bennett had put himself in the caregiver role for Ray-Ray out of necessity, but now there were adults to parent the boys and he could focus on being a kid.

She went to her knee in front of Bennett and looked at him, her hands firmly holding his upper arms.

"You have great plans for the weekend and the following week. We're not going to allow her to derail your joy. You have a family you can depend on. A family that will protect Ray-Ray and you."

His jaw was still tight. He stepped back and one of Lyrissa's hands slipped off his arm. But her other hand found the smaller one and held on, not letting him go.

Reno stepped next to her and put his hand on her shoulder. "Hey. He knows you have plans for the week. Great plans that you've been extremely excited about."

Lyrissa nodded. "Your job is to have fun and at the end of the week, come home and report back if the camp was as good as the hype." She pulled him to her and hugged him.

He was stiff at first but then awkwardly patted her. He wouldn't have done that a month ago.

Cooper came running down the pier. "Hey, Bennett. They're starting a new round. Are you still my partner?"

"I don't know. I'm thinking about going home."

"What? But you're staying the night. What happened?" Cooper came closer and lowered his voice. "Is it what Matt said about your mom? Don't let him get to you. He can be a jerk. I'll talk to my dad and make him leave."

"Don't make a scene. That's what my mom does, and I hate it. I just want to go home."

Cooper came closer and glanced at the two adults before turning his attention to Bennett.

"Hey, I get it. Did you know I'm adopted? I'm not really a Espinoza."

"Yes, you are." Reno didn't like that line of thought.

Cooper smiled. "Sorry, Tio. They are but I didn't grow up here. My mom had problems with that kind of stuff too and she started lying a lot. We don't have to talk about it. I just wanted you to know I understand."

Reno had always liked this kid, but he just lifted him up a level. Bridges would be proud of his son. Bennett didn't look convinced.

"If Ray-Ray needs you, I'll call." Lyrissa squeezed his hand. "I promise. You've been excited about camp. Don't let our mother take that from you. I did that too many times. If you stay with Cooper and go to camp, you'll be showing your brother how life should be lived."

He nodded. "Okay. But you'll call?"

"Yes. I promise."

He gave her a quick hug then turned to Cooper. "Come on, let's go beat them."

Lyrissa watched the boys run back to the pirate ship. Arms across her middle, she looked so alone. He wanted to pull her into his arms and shelter her from all the pain.

He reached out and waited for her to accept his offer. She looked down then glanced up. "I'm not good company right now."

"This is not about entertaining me. You need a friend. Let's walk on the beach since you don't want to go home. Or have you changed your mind? Is there somewhere you want to go?" he asked.

"I don't have anywhere else to go." She sighed and took his hand.

"As long as I'm around, you'll always have somewhere to go and someone to talk to. I've got your back. Always." She had his heart too, but that he kept to himself.

If all she needed from him was friendship, then that's what he would give her.

The waves rolled in and out. Her heart followed the rhythm and calmed down. They were far enough away that her breathing finally slowed to a normal level. Why was she letting it upset her? Nothing had actually happened. It was just based on what could have happened.

Even if her mother had perfect behavior, people would be watching and waiting for the worst. Including her. This was all her family would ever be known for.

"She doesn't reflect who you are. You know that, right?" Reno's gentle voice interrupted the downward spiral she was about to dive into.

She snorted. "In this town? I've been judged by my mother's actions my whole life."

"By some. Yes. But the people who really know you don't hold you up against her. More importantly, God doesn't judge you by your mother's actions."

She plopped down into the sand, and dug her toes in. She stared out into the horizon. Giant clouds billowed above the line that separated Earth from the sky. Dark blue and gold faded as the day slipped away. "My favorite thing about Port Del Mar was the sunsets. It might be the only thing I miss."

With a harrumph, he landed beside her. "Ouch. Good thing I have a tough hide."

It was safer not to respond.

"Hey. Don't let a few people ruin all the good. This is a great little town. Your dad and grand-mother are here."

She sighed. He wouldn't understand fighting to fit in. "You have a family that people adore. One's in law enforcement. One is a beloved mid-wife, and two others own the best bakery for miles. Then there's your mother. She is every-thing my mother is not. Even you. Mr. Run-to-the-Rescue-and-Ask-Questions-Later. You've always been popular."

He leaned forward, crossing his arms over his bent knees. "Most of us struggle at one point or another. When Dad died, my mother had to raise seven kids on her own. People felt sorry for us.

We were seen as charity cases. We were told to smile and be grateful even when it felt people were looking down on us. For some, it was more about showing how generous and wealthy they were. Look at us giving help to the poor Espinoza kids. People made comments that she shouldn't have had so many kids." He shrugged.

That had never crossed her mind. "I'm sorry. From my seat, it looked like you had everything."

He snorted. "On one level, I did. But I was also so worried that someone would figure out my secrets, I could never relax and be myself. I couldn't let anyone see the real me. It somehow became my job to keep everyone smiling."

"You're more than that. What about your happiness?" Heart racing, she reached out and touched his arm. "You're a good man."

Twisting, he looked away. "I'm not so sure. I've been pretending for so long." He turned back to her, and his eyes searched hers. "But with you I feel like I'm closer." His gaze lowered to her lips. *Oh. He is thinking about kissing me.*

Not wanting to give herself time to change her mind, she leaned forward and laid her hand gently on his cheek. She needed to be seen by him. To connect to him.

Eyes closed, she moved forward, and he met her. The touch was tentative at first. As soft as a butterfly landing then moving to another petal. He pressed his lips to hers to move back then came forward again.

She turned to get closer. Her other hand went to his shoulder. This was the closest she had ever felt to another human. Could she just stay here forever, wrapped up in his warmth?

He leaned back and caressed the side of her hair. "You're so beautiful. I'm not anchored to this town, you know."

Blinking, she tried to connect what he was saying to the present moment. Past the way he made her feel. Feelings like that were danger-ous. "What does that mean?"

"It means I could leave if I wanted to. I can do any sort of work."

There was no way she heard him right. "Are you saying you would leave Port Del Mar for me?"

"Yes."

"You can't do that. Pleasing other people can't be the reason you do something. And what about being a firefighter?"

"If it's someone you...really like and their happiness makes you happy, then what's the problem?" He shrugged and grinned. His thumb traced her jawline. "It would be good for me too. I'll always be the youngest Espinoza here. I might never pass that test. As much as I want to change the role I've played my whole life, I don't know if people will let me."

Dropping his hand, he gave her space to breathe. Leaning back on his palms, he stared out into the ocean. The reflection of the setting sun was fading. The last bit highlighted his strong profile.

"I'd recommend Houston or Austin," he said. "Somewhere close enough we can come home if they need us."

"Reno. You're moving too fast. I like you, but you're talking about moving away from the only home you've known because of me?" The tightness in her chest made it hard for her lungs to work. "Plans have to be carefully thought out, and groundwork needs to be laid. You can't just decide huge, big life-changing moves on impulse. After one kiss. No matter how great it was."

"So, you admit it was great?" His gaze moved across her face and his smile fell at her serious look. He went back to the safety of the ocean view. His jaw flexed. Was he upset with her?

She reached out and placed her hand over his in the warm sand. "You can't be serious about leaving Port Del Mar and your family."

"Why not? You don't want to stay because you feel people just see your mom when they look at you. Why can't I do the same? My family casts a big shadow too. It's not an impulse. It's been in my head a while now."

"I'm not sure why we're even talking about it. My family is a mess and the last thing I need is any romantic entanglement to bring more drama into my life. I like you, I really do. Can we just spend time together and be friends while I'm still in town?"

He stood and dusted the sand from his slacks. "I'll follow your lead."

He offered to help her up, but his beautiful smile didn't have the same warmth as earlier. Was she overanalyzing and messing up a good thing? He dived in without looking. Was she being overly cautious and methodical?

"It's getting late. Let's get you home." In silence, they walked down the beach to the pier. Music and laughter could still be heard.

Reno opened his truck door for her.

She paused and looked at the lights strung across the patio where the celebration was still going full force. Then back at Reno to thank him for a wonderful night.

Reno was watching his sister dance with her new husband. One side of his face was highlighted with the warm glow, emphasizing the beauty of his features. It left the other side deep in shadow.

Everyone hid parts of themselves. Parts that

weren't always easy to live with once they were revealed. She looked at the happy couple who were putting all their faith in love. That was terrifying.

"How do you think they have so much hope?" she asked. "Enzo already had one failed marriage. How do you think he's able to believe it will work this time? How does someone trust again? Like my father taking my mother back over and over." She was babbling and not making any sense. She didn't even understand her own mind.

"Your father is a man of strong faith and loyalty. I don't think he saw the damaged woman you see. He was fighting for the girl he fell in love with. As for Enzo? I don't know. I can only imagine he's seen a dark side of the world as an FBI agent. Coming home and turning his life over to God gave him a new outlook. I don't think it was easy. At one point, my sister thought she had lost him. Now they have everything they want because they trusted God and each other."

She pulled herself up into his truck and buckled her seat belt. He walked around and slipped into the driver's seat. "Reno. Thank you for getting me out of there. I'm sure you would rather be with your family instead of dealing with my drama."

"There was no real damage caused. Everyone was having a good time, and I don't think they noticed any problems before your dad and grandmother got her out of there."

"Only because of Elijah's help. I'm sure he didn't want a scene in his restaurant. That was so embarrassing. If no one noticed tonight, I'm sure they will hear about it tomorrow." She tilted her head back and closed her eyes.

"Elijah is not going to say anything. He's been there. He understands."

"Yeah, I remember his uncle. That man lived to cause scenes."

"You've been gone so you don't know, do you? Elijah is a recovering alcoholic. Everyone in town knew and a lot of people had written him off, including his in-laws. He lost his wife and oldest daughter for a while because of his drinking. He's been clean for about ten years. They've only been back together for a few years now."

"Seriously? Wow."

"He's someone who can help your dad."

She watched the landscape go by without seeing it. "I guess I get so caught up in how my family is so messed up, I see everyone else's as perfect." She sighed. "I'm also worried about the boys. They'll have to grow up in my mother's shadow like I did. There are already rumors about them. Should I stay?" Her brain was at war with her heart. Each answer had flaws, and each had benefits. But it came down to her living in Port Del Mar. The place she dreamed of escaping most of her life. "I can't. Not if my mother's here. I just can't deal with her and her legacy."

"You can get a place over the bridge. You'd be close enough to see the boys but not live with your mom. There are always options."

He was right. She didn't have to live on the ranch or even in Port Del Mar. She could take the full-time job and get an apartment in a town nearby. "I wish I had the type of faith you and my father have."

He laughed as he turned onto the dirt road going to her house, her dad's house. "Letting go of our fears and expectations to trust God fully is hard. My mom and your dad are great role models. You are too. Because of you I was able to find the faith to try for my dreams of being a firefighter again. You have it, you just have to trust."

They sat in silence until Reno sang along with the song on the radio. He winked at her. He made life seem so much easier than it was. How did he do that?

As he approached her father's house, he turned off his headlights. He parked in front of the porch and killed the engine. The phone between them vibrated. He flipped it over.

"It's a text from Elijah." His gaze scanned the

screen. "He put a few extra desserts in the back seat. And he said to tell you not to worry. Everything is fine and if anyone—he emphasized *anyone*—needs help, he is just a call away. He wants you to have his number."

The thought of Elijah De La Rosa offering her family help made her eyes burn. She blinked a few times to push the tears back. "That's very kind of him."

Reno tried to get the dessert in the back seat. "Oh man!" He lifted his hand. It was covered in whipped cream and chocolate shavings. He licked the majority of the cream off his fingers. "What a mess." With his other hand, he lifted the brown paper bag by its handles. The Painted Dolphin logo was stamped on the side. He peered inside. "Good news. I only took out the top pie." He licked his fingers. "Bad news. The top pie is a goner. Can I come inside to wash this off?"

She took the bag from him. "Let me have this before you deprive anyone of the good stuff. Come on. I'll see if Ray-Ray is still awake. This is his first night without his brother. He deserves a treat."

He followed her through the dark house. The silence was heavy. "Did you say they made it home?"

"Yes. Dad said he took Dee to Mew-Maw's

house. He put her in her old room and brought Ray-Ray home." She liked having Reno in the house. He made it feel so much safer, even with her mother around. She looked at her watch. "He is used to turning in early."

In the kitchen, she sat the bag on the table then turned on the light over the sink. He turned on the water, but nothing came out.

"Oh, sorry." She opened the door under the farm sink and dropped to her knees. "There was a leak and Dad didn't have time to fix it before we left so he just turned off the water." She popped back up, leaned across him and turned on the water. For a moment, they stared at each other. She was so close she could see all the details in his eyes, smell the clean fresh scent of him. Sea salt, leather and bonfires on the beach. She was too close.

Lifting her hands in the air, she took a step backward. "Ta-da! Modern wonders. Here." She handed him a towel then turned away before she kissed him again. "I'll get Ray-Ray. He'll think it a special treat to eat this late and with you."

Rushing up the spiral staircase, she counted to get her heart rate back to normal. She could not kiss him again. Once was a mistake; twice would be a disaster and it wouldn't be fair to him.

She came to the top of the landing and found the beds empty. All of them. The bottom bunk had been slept in. The sheets tossed aside. She checked in the bathroom. He wasn't there.

Leaning over the railing, she tried to stay calm as she called down to Reno. "He's not here. Ray-Ray's gone."

Chapter Thirteen

"Don't panic. He could be with your dad." Reno tried to reassure her as she ran for the hallway.

Reno thought through all the scenarios. Did he go to the barns? Or to Edith's house? That's where his mom was. That made sense. He grabbed the heavy-duty flashlight.

"He's not with Dad." She rushed back into the kitchen. "Should I call 911? Seriously, it seems like one emergency after another. I'm doing something wrong." A wild desperation burned in her eyes.

"You haven't done anything wrong. I'm sure he's close by."

A sleepy-eyed Mundo came into the kitchen behind her. "Yeah. He might be at Mew-Maw's. He had wanted to stay with his mother. But I said no. Then he wanted to get Benny and again I told him no. There is a slight chance he went to get his brother. They're used to walking everywhere. I should have slept upstairs with him. I knew he's never been away from Benny, but I thought this was good for him. I'm an idiot." Mundo was looking for something, digging through the drawers and moving things on the counter.

"No more than the rest of us. He needed me and I was hanging out on the beach." Guilt poured from her.

Reno put his arm around her and pulled her close for a second then let her go. He just needed to make contact to let her know he was here for her. "No one is to blame. We thought he was safe in his room. You were going to check on him. That's why we know he is missing this soon."

Mundo looked at the clock. "It hasn't been long at all." He now had a set of keys in his hand. "I'll drive slowly to Bridges's place. You go see if he went to his mom. If we don't find him between those two places, I'll let Bridges know he is missing."

Lyrissa made a whimper.

"Most of the time, kids are close by," he reassured her.

It took him by surprise when she reached up and touched his face. "You'll go with me?"

His heart was pounding. He covered her hand with his and intertwined their fingers. It felt so right. Making sure to smile, he lifted the big flashlight. "I'm ready. Let's go."

Her father headed out the front door. Reno paused at the back stoop. His heart tugged at him to speak to God. "Can I take a moment to cover us all in prayer? Is that okay?"

She squeezed his hand and nodded.

"Lord, we come to you in thanksgiving. We ask that you continue to protect Ray-Ray and all our family. We lift them up to you. Open our eyes and ears so we find him quickly. Let us tuck him safely into his bed. Open our hearts to your wisdom so we may help him with his fears and insecurities. In Your name we pray."

"Amen," Mundo said, then went through the door.

"Thank you. That was perfect." She was searching to the left while they walked. "When is he going to start trusting us? I should have been here instead of avoiding the house."

"Beating yourself up won't help." He scanned along the sides of the well-worn path to the barns with the flashlight. "He's most likely curled up with your mom."

She nodded. "Ray-Ray!" she called out again. A slight panic was on the edge of her voice. She gently pulled him to the barns but didn't remove her hand from his.

"Let's check the barns on the way to Mew-Maw's. He loves the horses." The barn door was open. "It was always my favorite place to hide when things got overwhelming."

He wanted to go back in time and hug little

Lyrissa. To let her know she wasn't alone. Flashlight high above his head, he scanned the loft then the stalls to the right. He lowered the flashlight and went deeper into the barn.

Lyrissa was right behind him. "Ray-Ray," she called out.

"Shhhh." They both jumped at the unexpected female voice coming from the last stall. "He's sleeping." Dee's voice was low and gravelly. Lyrissa dropped his hand and rushed to the opened stall.

Reno followed her and found Dee sitting against a stack of hay. Her youngest was snuggled against her chest. One arm around her neck the other around something small and furry. The orange kitten was curled up in his lap. It would have been an adorable scene if they weren't so frightened.

This was not good. He didn't want to startle them with a light in Dee's face, but he really wanted to check her pupils.

"Mom?" Bewilderment filled the one word. Lyrissa went to her knees next to her brother. "What are y'all doing out here?"

There was a deep hollowness in Dee's eyes and voice that had him alert. He eased down to the other side. "Dee, are you okay?" He gently touched her arm. Closing her lids, she sighed. Her skin was normal to the touch. Lips and fingers were a good color.

His own breath came a little easier. He needed to call Mundo but he wasn't sure of the situation yet.

"Momma. Open your eyes. What are you doing in the barn with Ray-Ray? Reno asked if you are okay. Are you?"

There was a long silence. Dee finally lifted her lids halfway and looked at Lyrissa. With a weak attempt at a smile, she nodded.

Then she shook her head. "No. That's a lie. I've told so many lies. I can't do this anymore." New tears followed a well-worn path of wetness. She had been crying for a while. A shaking hand reached for Lyrissa, then dropped.

"I'm so sorry, baby. I'm not okay. No." She looked down and caressed Ray-Ray's hair. "I was going to leave. Walk to town and get a ride. But this sweet baby found me. He said he was looking at the stars, talking to God like his dad taught him. Then he saw me leaving Mom's. He wanted to show me his kitten. I thought about taking him with me."

Her face relaxed and a real smile slipped in for a minute. "I couldn't. Mundo's such a good daddy. I should have brought the boys home to him as soon as I had them." She raised her chin and gazed at her daughter. "Why am I so selfish? Daddy would be so ashamed of me. I was supposed to go with him to Dallas, did you know that? But my friends asked me to go to the movies. I should have gone. He wouldn't have fallen asleep. People said he was drunk, but that wasn't true. He was just tired. I've always been so selfish."

Reno laid a hand on Dee's shoulder. There was so much pain in every word Dee spoke. Lyrissa's expression was tight. Had she known the story behind her grandfather's death? He had a gut feeling the family didn't really have open conversations.

Lyrissa moved closer and smoothed Dee's hair. It was a wild, tangled mess around her face. "Mew-Maw says your dad was the best. You were just a kid. It wasn't your fault. From the pictures I've seen and the stories I heard, he loved you very much. And we both know people prefer drama over the truth. I'm grateful you brought the boys home."

Dee's gaze went over his shoulder. "My daddy built this barn. This is where your father first told me he loved me. I thought the world was perfect that day and I would be all right even with Daddy gone. But it didn't last. Your dad deserves someone so much better than me. I had been clean for two months and tonight because that woman flirted with your dad, I gave in. Just one drink, you know, to take off the edge. I hate hurting."

Her chin fell forward as she studied the sleeping boy snuggled up to her. "I messed it up for

Mundo. Why do I do that? I had promised your dad I wouldn't drink. I've made so many promises to him and broke them all. He deserves someone better. So do you and the boys."

Lyrissa's phone vibrated. With a frown, she answered the call. "Mew-Maw?"

"Yes. I'm with her. We're in the barn." Her gaze darted from her mother to him. The vein in her neck pulsed harder. "She's fine. Ray-Ray followed her to the barn. He's asleep in her lap. Will you call Daddy for me and let him know. He's on the road, looking for Ray-Ray."

Blowing out a puff of air, Reno ran his hand through his hair. *Well, that problem is solved.*

He knew that Mundo had a worst-case scenario plan for Dee. Once he got here, Reno could focus on Lyrissa. She might play tough, but no one wanted to face this kind of trauma alone. Nor should they.

Lyrissa nodded. "Okay. I love you too." She slipped her phone in her back pocket. "Mom." It sounded as if she were about to cry. "Mew-Maw found your note. She said to tell you she loves you and she was very worried."

Tears fell down Dee's face. "No matter how hard I try, I always end up making it all worse. I'm tired of being the bad person in the family. You hate me."

"No. Mom." Lyrissa pulled her knees to her

chest and hugged them close. The kitten looked up and meowed but stayed in the center of them.

His heart ached to take her in his arms and remove all the pain from her life.

"I never thought it was you, Mom. It's an addiction. It wants to control you. But you're not alone. Please, let us find help for you." She glanced at Reno. Tears were falling. "Should we call someone?"

"Dee, it's a horrible place to feel like you have failed everyone you love. But there are people trained to help you. As soon as Mundo gets here, I think you should talk with him about how you want to get help."

She reached out with her free hand to him. "Yes. Please. You know where I can get help?"

Taking it, he nodded. "The most important thing to remember is you're not alone."

"Thank you." With her free arm, she hugged her sleeping son closer. "He said he loved me, and I was his mommy. He asked me to stay. He promised—" A sob interrupted her words. She swallowed and kissed the top of his head. "He promised to be a good boy if I stayed. But he's already a good boy." Letting go of Reno, she reached a hand out to Lyrissa. "I'm so sorry for embarrassing you. I wanted to be a good mom but I…" She hung her head.

"I love you. I just want you to be sober."

"Dee?" Mundo rushed into the barn, pausing for a second at the stall door. He was out of breath. Reno stood to give Mundo space. He joined her on the ground and pulled her into his arms. He held on to her and Ray-Ray as if he'd never let them go. "Sweetheart, are you okay?"

"No. I'm so sorry Mundo. I'm so sorry." She was sobbing now.

Lyrissa gently picked up the kitten and handed him to Reno. Purring, the orange fluffball curled up against him. Then she untangled Ray-Ray from her mother and lifted him onto her shoulder "I'm going to put him to bed."

Her little brother opened his eyes. "Mommy?"

"I'm right here, baby." She stood with Mundo's help. "Let me take him." She reached for her youngest son.

"My kitty. Please let me keep Butter."

Reno stroked the fluffball. "Butter? You named him?"

He nodded. "Mew-Maw said butter makes everything better. He makes me feel better. Can I keep him?"

They turned to Mundo. He had had a strict rule that cats belonged in the barns not the house. Mundo looked at Dee. "It's up to your mother. Can he keep the cat in the house?"

With watery eyes, she nodded. "That's a great

idea. She can keep you company and make you better while I'm at the hospital getting help."

Mundo rubbed the boy's back with one hand and held on to Dee with the other. "I agree. Butter has a new home. You'll have to take care of him. Like your mommy said, she's been sick so I'm taking her to the hospital."

"Mommy, you said you wouldn't leave," he cried.

Dee wiped her face again. "I'm going so the doctors can help fix me. I'll be back. Your daddy will take me so he can tell you where I'm at. It might be tonight or in a few days. Will you let us tuck you into bed in case he takes me tonight? Your sissy will stay with you."

"I want to go with you." He reached for his mother and hugged her tightly around the neck.

"You stay here and help Mew-Maw, okay? I promise I'll be back." Tears ran down her face. "Me and your daddy will take you to the house. I'll read a bedtime story. Then I have to leave as soon as they let me in so I can get better. I promise…" She took a deep breath. "I really promise that I'll come back. Can I tell you a bedtime story?"

He nodded.

Lyrissa patted his back. "I'll be in the house soon. Do you want me to sleep upstairs with you?"

"Will you? You won't leave? And Reno. Will he stay?" Ray-Ray asked.

His heart melted a little. No one had ever turned to him for support during challenging times. His throat burned. He would not cry. He wouldn't. One corner of his mouth flipped up, but he couldn't get to the other side without it feeling like a grimace.

Lyrissa shot him a quick glance. "I will be by your side all night. In the morning, we will go get Bennett."

"What about Reno?"

He looked at Lyrissa. She gave him a quick nod of approval. "I'm staying right here as long as you need me. In the morning, I'll take you and your brother for breakfast at my sisters' bakery." The kitten touched his face with its soft paw. "And we need to go to the feedstore and get Butter all the house supplies he needs to move from the barn to your room."

"Okay." He reached for the kitten and the orange bundle of fur almost leaped from Reno to Ray-Ray. "He already loves me." He pulled him close and smiled with his eyes closed as he stroked the top of the kitten's head. The purring filled the barn.

Mundo and Dee took Ray-Ray to the house. As soon as they were out of sight, Lyrissa collapsed on the barn floor. Without hesitation,

Reno rushed to her side and gathered her to him and surrounded her with his arms. Time had no measure as she sobbed.

He held her close and rocked her. Whispering words of care and support. He wasn't sure what he was telling her. He just wanted to fill the silence with comforting words.

Taking a deep breath, she pulled back and wiped her face. "I'm so sorry."

"Don't be. No reason to apologize." He wanted to pull her back into his arms and hide her from all the pain in her world, but she had made it clear that wasn't his job. "Like you've recently told me. Sometimes we need to be sad. She's finally willing to get help. That's good, right?"

With a sharp intake of breath, she swept the barn with her gaze. Her expression had grown hard as she put distance between them. She was isolating herself. "Where do we take her?"

Reno couldn't take it any longer. He reached for her and pulled her against his chest and held tight. She buried herself deeper into his arms. "Your dad has a plan. He already has a facility researched. He has one in Austin. In her current mental state, he might be able to get her in immediately. She'll be a priority. And she asked for help. That's huge, Lyrissa. As horrible as this night has been, it might be a blessing."

Sniffing, she leaned back. "Really? Daddy will be able to get her in tonight?"

"Probably. He had already spoken to her about it. He loves your mother, but he also knows the facts. If she's going to get better, she'll need professional help. I'm sure that's where he's taking her tonight."

The doors and windows rattled as the wind tried to push through. She stood. "I need to get myself together and into the house. They won't leave Ray-Ray alone and I need to go so they can get Mom to the center." She wiped her face with the top of her dress.

He wished he carried one of those old-fashioned handkerchiefs like his dad did. Or a bandanna. The urge to take care of her was so strong. He reached his hand out but she hesitated and slipped past him.

"I know it's asking a lot, but would you stay? I'm going to be upstairs with Ray-Ray, but I don't want us alone in the house. It's weird, but I…just feel so raw? I'll have to get Bennett in the morning and explain that Mom leaving is a good thing this time." Exhaustion shadowed her voice.

"Maybe let him go to camp. We can—" Before he could finish, her phone chimed.

"It's Mew-Maw." She answered and updated her grandmother. "Do you want me to come over?" She paused, listening. "Okay then. I'll see you in the morning. Mew-Maw, get some sleep. I love you."

Lyrissa hung up then tilted her head back and closed her eyes. "Dad called Mew-Maw. He'll be able to take her tonight. I'm so tired."

"Just like I told your mom. You're not alone. Are you ready to go to the house?"

With a nod from her, he led the way in the dark. He didn't offer his hand again. One rejection was all he was able to handle tonight.

It was too much. Lyrissa's emotions were all over the place and it hurt her heart and her mind. At this moment, she understood her mother's desire to numb herself. But that wouldn't help, obviously.

They stopped inside the kitchen. She didn't even remember walking to the house. When he had held her and let her cry, she felt safe enough to fall apart, like he could hold all the lost pieces until she was strong enough to pull them back together. That was dangerous. Holding his hand was off-limits.

"Lyrissa?" He said it as if he was repeating himself.

She blinked and looked up at him. Poor guy. His family was so wonderful. What did he think of hers? "I need to go upstairs." But she didn't move.

"I'm worried about you." He pushed her hair

back. It had to be a mess. Wanting to lean into his touch, she forced herself to step away.

He asked, "Do you want your grandmother to come over?"

"No. No. I'm fine."

He raised both brows.

"Okay. I'm not, but I will be. I never gave it thought, why she chose to feed her addiction."

He pulled a chair out. "Here, sit. I'll make tea." Reno put the kettle on the stove for hot water. He pulled her basket of teas out of the cabinet. "Which one do you want?"

How had she ever thought this man was shallow and irresponsible? He'd been the surprising anchor in the wild waves of this life. It was so tempting to cling to him and hold on for dear life.

Her father came down the stairs. Good timing. A great reminder that she couldn't afford a man-made shelter from this storm. Her dad would be focused on her mom. She'd have to take a page from his favorite book. Have faith that God had her and her family would get through this. She stood. "I need to go upstairs."

Her father shook his head. "She wants to stay with Ray-Ray for the next hour. He asked her to read all the books they had up there. When she finishes, I'm taking her to the house to pack a bag."

"What can I do to help?"

"Stay up there with him when we leave. Pick up Bennett in the morning and let him know what is happening."

"Of course, Daddy. I'll do whatever you need. Are you okay?" This man had been through so much and had given everything to his wife.

He hugged her. "Yes. My faith is strong that God has us. This is the first time she's ever admitted to needing help and willing to go to rehab on her own. I don't know what the future holds, but I have real hope." He patted her back then let go. "I'm going back upstairs. You take the next hour for yourself. I know this has been hard on you. I'm sorry we weren't the parents you deserved."

"Daddy." She hated that he ever thought she was disappointed in him.

He kissed her forehead. He glanced over at Reno waiting by the archway between the kitchen and living room. With a nod to the other man, he went back up the stairs to his wife and son.

Reno walked over to her and held out a warm cup of tea. After she took it, he went to the counter and picked up a second cup. She just stood there watching him. Was he real?

He took a sip. "Sit. Drink your tea and let me know what I can do to help."

"You know, when all this started, I was the

one helping you. Have you registered to retake the exam?"

"Aww. So, we're going to change the subject. Okay." He grinned at her. "I have. It's in about a week." He was staring into his tea. "It's not easy to ask for help, is it?"

"No. I think we all would rather be the hero than to be the one who needs saving." The silence between them was comforting as she sipped the soothing tea. "Is that why you want to be a first responder? You were great with my mother earlier. I froze. I didn't have a clue what to do, so I did nothing." She wanted to cry all over again. She brought the cup of tea up to her face and took a deep breath.

"I've had training. When something traumatic happens, if you have a plan then your mind will default to that. Your dad had a plan. That's reason he was able to get her moving. He was prepared."

"He was." She was so proud of her father tonight. "She's going to get the help she needs because he never lost faith." She closed her eyes and took another slow sip of her tea. The lemon-balm-and-lavender mix was her favorite. "You don't have to stay the night. Driving back over in the morning will be fine. It's been a long day for you."

"I'm good."

"Oh." She sat up and gaped at him. "Your sister's wedding. They must be missing you."

"Nope. They're good. I texted Mom to let her know I took you home. She said not to worry about coming back to the reception." He laid the phone on the table. "I need to let her know I'm staying here. I'll let Bridges know we'll be picking Bennett up in the morning."

"I feel horrible that you missed any family moments."

He laughed. "Then I must thank you. The only moment I missed was cleaning duty. Which I've done a million times, so I have credit." He took a sip, then his gaze went up to the loft. "What do you want me to tell Mom about why I'm staying tonight? She'll ask and not let it go until I give her an answer."

"That my mom has finally agreed to go to rehab. I don't think the rest is anyone's business outside of our family." Lifting her cup, she took a slow sip. "This is my favorite tea. Thank you. It has helped to calm my nerves and settle my brain."

He reached for her father's bible, which sat on the table. It was here in the hub of the house unless he was meditating in prayer. "My mother has verses for everything this world will throw at you. There's one in Philippians she uses a great deal." He flipped through the well-loved and used leather bible with confidence and knowledge.

"Here it is, 4:8–9. 'Finally, brethren, whatsoever things are true, whatsoever things are honest, whatsoever things are just, whatsoever things are pure, whatsoever things are lovely, whatsoever things are of good report; if there be any virtue, and if there be any praise, think on these things. Those things, which ye have both learned and received, and heard, and seen in me, do: and the God of peace shall be with you.'"

At first, she didn't really understand. It wasn't one of the obvious verses that she expected. She took the time to process each word. "That's candidly beautiful. It's like a warning but full of hope all at the same time. God knows the world is a mix of beauty and brutality. It's God who can give us peace in the messiness of life."

They sat in prayerful silence. She finished her tea and stood to take the cup to the sink. "Thank you, Reno. That really helped."

"No problem. Happy I could help. Where am I sleeping? The sofa looks good."

"Are you sure you want to stay? I think you're longer than the couch."

He laughed. "I'm the youngest of seven kids. I can sleep anywhere. Just give me a blanket and pillow and I'm good."

"I can do that." She went to the linen closet

and pulled out the extra bedding. Then she went to the sofa and made it up. She snapped the sheet open, then tucked it under the cushion. "Thank you so much for doing this. It's going to be so much easier to explain this all to Bennett with you there. The boys have really connected to you." It was also going to make her feel safer, but she didn't want to spend any time analyzing that.

"I'm glad I can help. Your brothers have become special to me. What I can't believe is your father has agreed to let a cat live in his house."

After fluffing the pillow, she spread the top sheet. "I love the way he let Mom be the hero. It'll help the boys while she's gone."

He nodded. "I hope I can be at least half as good a man as him."

She stopped fussing with the bedding. "What? Do you really think you're not?"

He shrugged. "I feel like I lied my way through life, and no one ever took me seriously. They still don't."

"You thought you were protecting the people you love from worry and stress. You didn't lie, just hid what you saw as flaws. You put your family's feelings above your own. You're a good man, Reno."

The sofa was now a makeshift bed. Hands on her hips, she scanned the room. Not a single thing left to distract her.

Reno stood in front of her. "Lyrissa? Talk to me. What's going on in that beautiful brain of yours?"

She shook her head. "I don't want to think about it. But...what if she changes her mind when it gets hard? It's not going to be easy to undo everything from the last twenty or thirty years."

He took both of her hands and sat her down in the chair. He sat across from her on the coffee table. "*You* will be okay. Is it going to be a happy ending with your mom?" He shrugged. "There is no telling. But she has a dedicated support system. The one thing I know for certain is you have the boys, your father and grandmother, and they have you." There was a longing in his gaze that made her uncomfortable. "I want to be here for you too if you let me."

She sat back and shook her head. "That's not fair to you."

"I can decide that. Are you sure it's not that you're scared to rely on someone else? On me? You think I'm untrustworthy. Too much like your mother?" His eyes held her gaze.

She had to close her eyes to break the intense contact. She wanted to reach out and hold on to him, but he was right. That would take a leap of faith she didn't have the courage for. She settled by touching his cheek with her hand. "I'm sorry I ever thought you were anything like my mother. You are a man of honor and can be counted on. But there is so much up in the air right now. I don't even know if I'll still be here in the fall."

He stood and moved away from her, then sat on the opposite chair. "Life's hard enough. No reason you should have to do it alone."

Breathing easier now that she had more space, she leaned back in her chair. "Can we just sit here until they leave. Then I'll go upstairs."

"As long as you need me and want me here, I'm not going anywhere." He looked around. "Do you want me to put on one of your dad's old records? We can play gin rummy."

"I'd like that." She settled into the oversize chair covered in a quilt made by her great-grandmother. The soft sounds coming from one of her father's favorite vinyls wrapped around her. Tilting her head back, she closed her eyes and took a few deep breaths.

They played a few rounds, but her mind wasn't on the game.

"Hey. You want me to look at the sink? I can have it fixed before your dad gets back."

She curled up tighter in her little nest. "That would be great. Thank you."

He flipped the record then went into the kitchen. She snuggled deeper into her great-grandmother's quilt and shut out the world. Reno made it easy to breathe and forget the stress.

She didn't have the right to feel this comforted with all the wrong going on in her family. Rolling her head to the side, she peeked into the next room where she heard a metallic clink. Reno was under the sink. She grinned. He might be always looking for a good time and finding ways to make others laugh, but he had a heart to serve others.

Comparing him to her mother had been blatantly wrong. One day, he would make a perfect husband for some incredibly happy woman. New tears threatened to fall, but not for her family this time. She knew she had to let Reno go. It was the only right thing to do for him.

It would be wrong to tie such a beautiful human to the train wreck of her life.

Chapter Fourteen

Everyone in Reno's truck sat very quietly, each lost in their own thoughts. He cleared his throat. "So, this doesn't mean you shouldn't go to camp with Cooper tomorrow morning."

Lyrissa nodded. "That's true, Bennett. I promise we'll call you if anything major happens. But at this point, there is nothing for you to do. She'll be safe in rehab, getting healthy."

"But what about Ray-Ray? He needs me."

Twisting in her seat, Lyrissa reached her hand out to him. "You're not alone anymore. You both have Daddy, Mew-Maw and me. Even Reno is here. You were excited about the camp. Show Ray-Ray how to carry on with the good things in life. Go to camp."

He gave her a nod but doubt still filled his eyes. She faced forward and discreetly wiped a tear away.

Reno glanced up to check on the boys. In the rearview mirror, they were holding hands. Ray-Ray nodded in agreement. "You wanted to go to camp. You should go. Lyrissa said she'd sleep upstairs with me until you get back."

These boys were too old for how young they were. "It's good that y'all are talking about it," Reno told them. "My brother said we can call him anytime today to let them know. Do what feels right." He found a parking spot on the boardwalk. It was thick with tourists, so they'd have to walk a few blocks to his sisters' bakery. "Ready for the best empanadas you've ever eaten?"

"Can I have a doughnut with chocolate milk?" Ray-Ray asked.

"Yes. But I'm also ordering a few different empanadas. You have to at least try one. They might change your whole outlook on life."

He helped Ray-Ray out of his truck and pointed out someone flying a kite. "Ray-Ray and I can pick up some kites or even try to make one while you're at camp. As soon as you get back, we'll come to the beach and fly them."

The boys were excited and picked their favorite ones that were in the air and guessed how high they were. Lyrissa stepped out from his truck.

With a smile that didn't look at all natural, she joined them. "Just talked to Dad." She stood between the boys and hugged them to her side.

"Mom is checked in and she likes the place. He said it's really nice and she has pictures of us that are important to her. He'll be on his way home soon. We should pick up some of their freshly made cuernitos pan dulce."

Bennett gazed up. "A sweet bread?"

"Very good. Yes, it's light and flaky like a croissant. I'll stuff them with my chicken salad."

"We can grab a dessert too," Reno said as he started walking toward his sisters' shop. On the right side of the sidewalk, huge boulders protected the street from the ocean. Below on the sandy beach, families enjoyed the sun and surf. Across the street on his left were the historic storefronts. All the repairs from the last hurricane were complete.

Ray-Ray was walking between him and Lyrissa. It took him by surprise when the small fingers found his. Looking down, he found Ray-Ray watching the beach. One little hand in his, the other in Lyrissa's.

That is not my heart melting. Nope, it isn't. He blew out a puff of air. *This kid.* For the first time in his whole life, he truly longed for a family. Being a father. The only problem was he could only see Lyrissa as the mother.

Bennett walked a few steps ahead, pointing birds out to his little brother.

"Can we feed them?"

"Only if you want to be attacked," Reno chuckled.

Lyrissa shook her head, but she was grinning. "One time I ran screaming from the beach. Hollering that the birds were going to kill me. I'll never live it down."

Someone honked and waved as they drove past. Ray-Ray let go of his hand and waved back. "People are so nice here. I like it. I hope we get to stay."

Bennett looked at them. Worry in his eyes.

"This is our home now. We're family. Right?" His voice soft. "I mean, we're used to moving. It's no big deal."

"It is a big deal. This is your forever family home." Lyrissa looked a little teary eyed.

He tried to think of a joke that would make her smile.

She looked at him, then narrowed her eyes as if she could read his thoughts. "This is good. It's okay to be a little sad. We have each other and God has us."

She knew him too well. He nodded.

The air was humid. But a cool breeze came off the gulf. He loved the Texas coast. Walking with Lyrissa and the boys felt good deep in his core. Anyone who didn't know better would see a family walking and enjoying the day.

His heart longed for this. To be a family with

Lyrissa. But she wasn't in the same place as him. *God, what do I do with these feelings?*

Another car honked. He waved without really looking. He got everyone safely across the street and held the door open for them.

"*Mijo.*" His oldest sister greeting them from behind the counter. "What a beautiful little family you have here."

He ignored the family comment. "I'm surprised to see you. The wedding kept you up way past your bedtime. I thought you'd have employees covering the shop this morning." He had hoped.

He loved his sisters, he did, but sometimes they were too much. The word *boundary* was not in their vocabularies.

"Oh, I did sleep in. Came in late. Josefina won't be coming in today. I'm taking tomorrow off. Now—" her gaze slipped to the boys "—tell me what brings you in this morning?"

Bennett and Ray-Ray stood close to Lyrissa, almost behind her. "I promised them the best empanadas ever." He leaned over the counter and spoke in a dramatic stage whisper. "They have never eaten them. You were out the last time we were here."

"We'll have to fix that." She went to the back of the store and returned with a platter of assorted pastries. "Come sit in the back booth." After placing the tray of goodies on the table, his sister turned to the boys and hugged each one of them. Holding the oldest for a bit longer, she whispered, "Being the big brother is a heavy burden, but you're not alone now."

Then she wrapped her arms around Lyrissa. "You have always been in our prayers. We don't understand God's timing and there is the slight problem of free will." She grinned. "If people would just listen to their elders, the world would be a place full of grace." She hit Reno's shoulder with the back of her hand.

He kissed his much-shorter sister. "Yes. If the world followed all your words of wisdom, all the people would live in joy and harmony."

"Oh, you. You're such a charmer. Some girl is going to be treated right when you decide to settle down." His sister had the audacity to wink at Lyrissa. "I'm going to the back to make sure your father gets his favorites. We ran out of the cinnamon churro empanadas faster than usual."

"Your sister is amazing." Lyrissa shook her head. "You know how blessed you are, don't you?"

He nodded, even though he took them for granted way too often. "I do. You know they've considered you family since you came home with Savannah after school."

She looked up at him, her eyes full of wonderment. "I was so busy listening to the negative gossip in town, I missed the people supporting me. Their numbers are much bigger than I imagined. I wasted so much time on the wrong people. Does that make me self-centered?"

"Human." He looked to the rustic wood beams above them, the colorful *papel picado* with intricate designs cut from tissue paper brightened the shop. "I think the correct word you are looking for is *human*. We tend to focus on the negative. I must admit I've fallen into the same trap more than once."

She took a bite of a pumpkin empanada and gave a little moan with her eyes closed. "This is so good." Lids opened, she made eye contact with him. "You don't."

"I don't what?" He had totally lost track of what they were discussing.

"Focus on the negative. You always have a smile. No matter what is going on, you're trying to make everyone else laugh."

The doors to the back swung behind his sister. "It's because I focus on the negative that I'm trying to distract the people around me. I hate seeing the ones I love sad. In my world, everyone would be happy."

He'd gotten too good at hiding his real emotions. Buried them so deep, it was impossible to reach them. He wasn't sure he would be able to express them clearly anymore. It was too raw.

She covered his bicep with her hand. Her gaze searched his. "I think we've all underestimated you. Your well runs much deeper than you let your family believe."

He shrugged, not really enjoying this line of questioning. "My family deserve the best and worrying about me is not how they should spend their time."

"They love you."

But he wanted her to love him. That wasn't going to happen. "Who needs more chocolate milk?"

"I do!" Ray-Ray lifted his hand high above his head. "Bennett too."

Needing space, he moved to the large glass front cooler. Fingers brushed the back of his hand. Maddy.

"Reno." She laughed and tucked a loose strand of hair behind her ear. Lowering her lashes briefly, she then lifted her chin and blinked at him. Smiling. "Imagine meeting you here."

He frowned. "At my sisters' bakery?"

"I know that's silly. I was teasing. I'd been wanting to see you. You left the wedding early before I could claim my dance."

"I took Lyrissa home." He glanced at the chocolate milk in the refrigerator. How to grab the bottles and run without being rude.

She was still talking as she blocked the door.

"I loved dancing with you back in the day. We had such a good time. With everything that's happened, I could really use some of the classic Reno fun and forget the past few years."

He tilted his head and studied her. No memories of them dancing came to mind. They had hung out with groups of friends, but he didn't remember interacting with her one-on-one. "I'm sorry, Maddy. Lyrissa and the boys are waiting. The church has an active singles group. Have you connected with them since you came back to town?"

Something harsh flashed in her eyes. Surprised, he stepped back. She followed him and in a gritty whisper said, "Careful you aren't pulled back into her drama. After using you up she'll be gone. Just like in high school. I'm still not buying that oldest is her mother's."

For a moment he was too shocked to say anything. Taking a deep breath, he shook his head. "We aren't high school kids any longer and I don't appreciate you talking about Lyrissa or Bennett like that. They're important to me."

"You can't be serious." She stepped closer, her voice a harsh whisper. Eyes wide, she stared at him. He moved back. Her hand went to his arm to hold him in place. "Did you see her mom create a scene all because my mom just wanted to dance with Mundo?"

"Maybe she…" He stopped himself from saying anything else. It didn't matter. "Like I said, we aren't in high school any longer. I've got to go."

Her grip tightened. All the years of being the nice guy and putting everyone at ease warred with getting as far away from her as possible.

She wasn't getting the hint and stepped full-on into his space. "Reno, please. You'll end up just like Mundo if you're not careful. He wasted his whole life on a woman who doesn't deserve him. Is that what you want? To look back on a life of regret with wasted time?"

He broke contact and glared at her. "Maddy, pettiness doesn't suit you. But I agree our time is too precious to hang out with negative people. Bye, Maddy." Reno was not going to allow her to take any more of his.

He stepped around her and grabbed two chocolate milks, then walked back to the table without a backward glance. Lyrissa met his gaze. A question in her eyes. She glanced at Maddy. "Everything okay?"

He did what he was good at—smiled. An easy, comfortable smile. "Yep." He looked at the boys. "So, are these the best things ever?"

"I want to eat a hundred of them," Ray-Ray cried.

Reno picked one up. "They have always made a rough day smoother. My sisters claim that my mom gave them secret ingredients. I've tried to watch them, but they always know and wait until no one is looking. I suspect it's a bit of love and hope."

Bennett scoffed. "Those aren't real ingredients."

Ray-Ray wiggled in excitement. "Those are real ingredients."

Lyrissa laughed. "It does make the day feel better and the sunshine brighter. I think you're on to something about the hope."

They made eye contact above the boys. For a long moment, they stared at each other and all the worries crowding his head disappeared. She leaned in close and put her hand over his. Every instinct screamed to move closer.

"Reno, this morning I couldn't have imagined smiling today, let alone laughing. Now I feel hope and love all around me. You do have a true gift."

She reached up and cupped his face. Every muscle locked in place. His lungs froze. Not a single breath went in or out. She dropped her hand and sat back. "Thank you."

After a few slow heartbeats he managed, "De nada."

A longing in him yelled to move in and kiss her. Just one sweet kiss. He sighed. Not the time, the place or the girl.

He was still the guy who made everyone smile. The desire to be more ate at him. He wanted to love her and be loved by her. He was in so much trouble.

For now, knowing he helped bring light back into her beautiful eyes was enough. It had to be.

Ugh. She did it again. Where was her self-control? With a shake of her head, she cleared her thoughts. "Sorry. That was weird."

He opened his mouth, but her phone went off. Pressing his lips closed, he leaned back.

She was just saved by her ringtone.

"Mew-Maw?" he asked, recognizing the theme song of *Bonanza*.

With a nod, she answered. "Hey, Mew-Maw." Listening, her gaze went to her brothers. "Do y'all want to go riding out to the north pasture with Mew-Maw?"

Ray-Ray jumped up on the bench. "Yes! Yes!"

Bennett was much more subdued, but he nodded. "I'd like that."

"We're at the bakery with Reno. So, we'll meet you at the barn in a bit." After disconnecting the call, Lyrissa pulled Bennett close and rested her cheek on top of his head. "Thank you. She needs to spend time with us."

The boy leaned into her for a quick minute and hugged her back. She savored the moment.

When she looked up, Reno was giving her a knowing smile.

Bennett tilted his chin as if he hadn't needed that hug and reassurance from his big sister.

Reno patted him on the shoulder. "It's a good start to the day."

The back corner booth was separated a bit from the general sitting area. Reno opened one of the bottles of chocolate milk and handed it to Ray-Ray. "You are sitting in the Espinoza special booth. This is reserved for family."

He looked at Lyrissa. "Speaking of family, my sister works at a clinic that has family counselors and connections to support groups through the church."

Lyrissa nodded. "Mew-Maw used to have the belief that you kept any problems in-house and didn't waste time talking about feelings." She held out her hands to both the boys and they held on to her as if she was a true lifeline. "She has changed her mind and would be willing to go as a family. Will y'all go with me?" she asked the boys. Ray-Ray agreed, not really understanding what was going on.

Reno opened the other bottle of chocolate milk and handed it to Bennett. "Your mother's addiction doesn't just turn her life upside down. It affects the whole family."

Bennett played with the corner of his pastry. "Will she come home?" he asked with his head down.

"Honestly, we don't know. I hope she will, but either way we need to make sure we are okay and living the life God has for us."

Bennett looked across the table at his little brother. "If it helps Ray-Ray, I'll do it."

Lyrissa's heart twisted at the pain they were going through. The desire to comfort them was so powerful it hurt. She wanted to make their world better.

She glanced at Reno. That's why he worked so hard to make the people around him smile. He had a huge heart and loved his people deeply.

The youngest dipped his fingers in the chocolate milk then put his eye against the opening and picked it up like a telescope. Reno gently placed the bottle back on the table and gave the little guy a napkin to wipe his face.

"Yep, the five-year-old is over this serious talk of support groups and healing," Reno chuckled. "I totally identify with being the youngest and totally bored with a family discussion."

He glanced at Lyrissa. She nodded. "I think we're done eating."

"Can we get a kite?" Ray-Ray lifted his bottle of chocolate milk as if it were flying.

Gently taking it from him, Reno grinned. "How about we walk across the street to the beach. We can look at the birds and kites before we leave for the ranch."

Lyrissa gave Reno a grateful smile. "Now that sounds like a wonderful idea."

"Great." He stood and helped Ray-Ray out. "Let me get a box from my sister so we can take the rest of the pastries home."

Lyrissa ran one hand through Ray-Ray's messy hair, attempting to tame it back into place. "Reno, do you mind going ahead with the boys? I'll take care of the food. I also need to tell your sisters thank you."

"Yay! The beach." Ray-Ray jumped then took off running.

Bennett stopped him and held his hand. "We have to wait for Reno."

Laughing, Reno took Ray-Ray's other hand. But as Bennett opened the door, Maddy got up from her table and made a beeline toward Lyrissa. He paused and looked at Lyrissa, then turned away from her and spoke to someone on the patio.

Through the window, she saw Jazz, Elijah's wife, with their daughter. The boys joined them, and Reno went back in.

Maddy touched her arm. "I know what you're doing. Just like your mom."

Lyrissa blinked. Had she heard her correctly? Was this really happening?

She had her head down and she spoke low.

"And if you care for Reno, you won't cling to him and drag him down with your sinking ship."

"Maddy." Reno was at her side.

"Reno." Maddy smiled, but it was tight. "I'm setting the record straight. We all know her mother is a walking disaster who ruined Mundo's life."

Taking a deep breath, Lyrissa placed a hand on his arm and gave him a quick glance.

He got the message. Stopping a few feet away, he put his hands in his pockets and pressed his lips together.

She faced Maddy. "My parents' relationship is between them and God. And Reno is an adult. He can take care of himself."

Maddy clasped her hands in front of her chest and lowered her chin as if being obedient. "I believe it's our duty to speak the truth and hold people accountable. Reno is a good man, and he deserves someone looking after his best interest."

Reno frowned. The expression foreign on his face. He was very unhappy, and Lyrissa didn't like that at all.

Before she could say anything to him, he glared at Maddy. "This is the reason she avoids town." He turned to her with guilt and pain in his eyes. "I'm sorry I brought you into town."

Lifting her chin, she smiled a calm, quiet smile at him. "It's okay. Really."

Looking a little confused, he paused.

Ignoring Maddy, she met his beautiful, warm gaze. "Honesty can be a fickle excuse for people to be mean and rude."

Then she turned to Maddy. Her voice was strong and serene. She lifted three fingers. "*Is* it the truth? Is it kind, and is it helpful? And by helpful, I mean, is it asked for and will it make a difference? I recommend that you take a long look in the mirror and start there. Not that you listen to others, but that's my advice to you."

Maddy leaned back with shock on her face. In the past, all the stabs she had made at Lyrissa had never been returned. In shame and embarrassment, Lyrissa had walked away. Not today.

She didn't need him to intervene. "Is there anything else I can help you with?"

"No, I'm good." Maddy went to her table, picked up her bag and walked out the door.

They stood shoulder to shoulder as they watched the woman leave.

Margarita came through the swinging doors. "These are your father's favorites." She put a white box on the counter. "On the house. Let him know we're lifting him up in prayer and if he needs anything else to let us know. We've got him covered from babysitting to food."

"I will. And I can't thank you enough for all your support. Not just today, but for as long as I can remember your family has been there for me."

"Para eso esta la familia." Margarita said it so casually, as if being a part of the family was a given. There was a huge lump in Lyrissa's throat. She smiled and nodded because words were impossible.

Reno hugged his sister, kissing her on the top of her head. She handed him an empty white box. He went to the table and packed what was left then turned to Lyrissa. "Ready to check out some kites and birds?"

"I am. Looking forward to riding with Mew-Maw and the boys too. You'll join us?" She wanted to bite her tongue. Why did she keep sending him mixed messages? She should make an excuse and take it back. Maybe he would say no.

He paused. Had she just invited him to spend more time with her? He grinned. She had. "Love too. Lyrissa, I'm so sorry about—"

She held her hand up and shook her head. "Don't. I've been hiding too long. I have way too many friends in Port Del Mar to stay away. I'm not going to let her make me ashamed of my family."

His chest burned with pride for her. She was so amazing, and she didn't even see it. If she would let him, he would find a million different ways to show her the woman he saw.

For now, he needed to act cool. With a nod, he went to the door but before he could open it, her phone rang again. Concern flashed across her face before she brought it to her ear. His whole body went tight, then she smiled. "Hello to you too."

He released his breath. It wasn't bad news.

"Yes. They did. I told them I'd let them know by Wednesday. Yea, but I have three other offers too." She paused. "I know, right? I had some family stuff come up. But it's nice to be wanted." She listened to the speaker. "Okay. I'll let you know. Thanks for calling."

She put her phone away then headed to the door. He paused before he pulled the door open. "You got a job offer on a Saturday?"

"No. I got it yesterday morning. That was a friend from college. She works in the district and when she heard I was offered the job, she called to encourage me to take it. It's in Missouri."

Rocks hit the bottom of his gut hard. "So, you're going back?"

"I don't know." She shrugged as if his whole world wasn't teetering on the edge of a canyon.

"I have an offer in Dallas and one in San Antonio."

He wanted to ask why she hadn't told him, but that sounded childish. Pressing his lips together, he bit back any pleading to make her stay or at least take the one in San Antonio. That was close enough for a day trip.

She raised an eyebrow in question.

He frowned. "What?"

Her gaze went over his shoulder.

Oh. Right. He was blocking the door. He pulled the door open and waited for her to go through. Clearing his throat, he tried to sound neutral. "What are you going to do?"

Not knowing the turmoil going on in his head, she gave a low sigh. "I was leaning toward the Dallas one. It's my dream job, but after last night I don't know."

"Like we told Bennett. You have some time. Don't rush it and don't let a sense of obligation make you do something that will steal who you are." *But please stay close or let me visit.*

She nodded. "Everyone is full of great advice today. I really don't know what I should do."

Face to the sun, she walked past him.

For a moment he couldn't breathe. She was beautiful. The world should be hers. "Pray and focus on what feels right."

She gave him a weak smile. "I'm just as clueless about that. Ready to get the boys?"

He was ready for whatever she wanted to do. Pointing to where they sat, he said, "Lead the way."

Chapter Fifteen

After church, the Espinoza family had invited her family to join them for lunch. It was loud and welcoming. Ray-Ray couldn't be separated from his new friends. They would be starting kindergarten in the fall with him.

Her heart was overflowing with watching her family connect with the community. They would need all this support when or if Dee came home.

Mew-Maw hugged Reno's mother. Her grand-mother stood a good foot over woman. "Thank you for a great lunch. I need to be heading back to the ranch." She turned to Bennett. "Are you going back to the ranch or staying and going to camp with Cooper?"

"Is it okay if I stay?"

Kids, including Ray-Ray, ran though the kitchen again to the back door.

"Of course. Go. Join your friends." He hugged each of them then ran off.

Lyrissa laughed. "I always loved the energy

at your home when I visited Savannah. But it seems ever more…"

"Bonkers? Chaotic?" Reno smiled as he tossed an apple to a tall boy who came around the corner.

"Not exactly. You love being surrounded by all your nieces and nephews." It wasn't a question. It was obvious. He loved being in the middle of his big family. He adored the kids. Someday, he'd be a great father.

His mother laughed. "Most of the time, he runs around with them. It's nice to see him acting like an adult. You've been an enormous influence on him."

"*Mami!*" He was turning red.

Mundo patted him on the shoulder. "Lyrissa has always been the most adult in our family. Too much so. He's been a good influence on her too." He turned to Reno. "Are you sure you can bring her home? If it's too much trouble, I can come back into town to pick her up."

Reno smiled. "I really appreciate her helping with my test. It's the least I can do. I'll bring her home early. I know she has work in the morning."

Her father and grandmother went out the back to get Ray-Ray and say goodbye to everyone. His mother grinned at them. "Y'all can work in the front living room. It will be quiet." She followed the others out.

"Why does it feel like we're being set up?" she asked.

"Because we are. Under all that sweetness, a stubborn streak runs deep." They went into the living room. He looked around, rubbing his hands on his jeans.

She gathered the material and books she brought. "Why don't we go outside? The front porch looks empty."

He nodded but didn't say anything. They settled in on the porch swing, the papers between them. She wasn't used to a silent Reno. "What's wrong? Are you feeling, okay?"

He took a deep breath. "I'm taking the test in a few days. I don't know if I'm ready." He snorted. "I might never be ready."

She leaned over and took his hand. "You've worked so hard. You're more than ready."

An uncharacteristic scowl pulled at his mouth. He leaned back and crossed his arms over his chest. "I've worked hard before and learned it was a waste of time." His tone had a sharp defensive edge to it.

"What happened?" She waited. He looked off in the distance. After a long, silent moment, he sighed. "In the sixth grade we had to write an essay that could be entered into a contest for the local animal shelter. I poured everything I had into that paper. It was about my dog being my best friend after my dad died. I went over that paper so many times. I wanted it to be perfect. I stayed in while everyone else was outside playing. I got to school early and sat in the bleachers looking for every mistake. I found them too. I was so proud I went to class early to give it to Mr. Poole. I knew it was going to win the contest. It would be published in the newspaper."

He looked away, his jaw flexing.

"Reno?" She moved closer and put her hand on his arm.

"He said it could have been a good paper if I had tried harder. He said being lazy with spelling and grammar would stop people from seeing my story. He gave me a seventy and didn't enter it in the contest. Hard work does not guarantee success."

She wanted to pull him into her arms. She also wanted to find that teacher and give him a good lecture about learning disabilities.

Instead, she nodded. "You're right. I misspoke. Learning disabilities can be huge hurdles and you have to work twice as hard to just do the bare minimum. But this time you asked for help. You have strategies in place. Take your time. Use the process that works for you. Believe you can." She reached for his hand. "You've got this. Either way, I'm proud of you for putting yourself out there. The world needs more first responders like you. You deserve the best and they deserve you."

He cupped her face and leaned in. "You do too. You've helped me get closer to my dream. Closer than I've ever thought possible." His throat worked as if he was about to say something that was difficult to get out.

"Lyrissa, let me take you out on a date. A real date and show you what a good relationship could be between us. I want to be there for you."

No. No. No. She tried to smile as she shook her head. "You're a protector. You need someone to rescue. That's what you see in me. My family is a fire you're not responsible for. Your energy and love need to go to someone who can return it. I don't think I can."

She stood before she leaned into him and did what she really wanted to do. Hug him close and never let him go.

"You're ready for your test. I need to go. Bye." *I love you* almost slipped out. It had to be buried. Saying it aloud wouldn't be fair to him. Port Del Mar was his home. His family was here. Her future was far from here.

She rushed down the steps then realized she didn't have her car. He was supposed to take her home. Frozen, she just stood there with her back to him.

"I'll get Bridges." His words were followed by the screen door shutting.

She wanted to say *No, it's alright. You can take me home.* But right now was not the time to be locked in a car with him. It didn't take long for his big brother to come out.

"Hey, hear you need a ride home." Bridges joined her.

Unable to speak, she nodded then followed him to his truck. Once inside, she glanced over her shoulder. Reno stood on the top step, tall and handsome, looking as if he might chase after her.

Was she making a mistake walking away or was she being smart?

The tears started falling. She bit the inside of her mouth to stop any sobbing, but the tears fell anyway. Her throat burned from holding in the yelling she craved to do.

Bridges stopped at her father's house. "Lyrissa, is there anything I can do? Are you okay? Well, obviously you're not. Do I need to have a man-to-man with my baby brother? He's a good guy but he's not the most mature when it comes to relationships."

She smiled. Poor Reno. Everyone always assumed he was the one who messed up. "I'm good. It's not Reno's fault," she managed to say.

"Thanks for the ride." She swung her bag over her shoulder and turned to the house. Then she stopped.

Mew-Maw was sitting on the swing. Was she waiting for her? Had something happened? With a smile, her grandmother stood and waved to Bridges as if letting him know she had it from here. He drove away.

The woman who raised her tilted her head and arched an eyebrow. She opened her arms and waited.

Pulling in a deep breath, she wanted to rush to the porch. But the earth shifted under her boots, making it difficult to move forward. It was like walking through deep sand. It shifted, not letting her get traction. Her entire world was unstable, and she didn't know what to do.

As a teenager, she ran as far away as she could. Was there anywhere far enough to escape a broken heart? The worst part? It was all her fault.

"Mew-Maw." She made it to the steps.

"Hey, cowgirl."

"Why are you here?"

"My sweet child, you're hurting."

"You always said to pull up your boots and move forward. No sense in wallowing. It's a waste of time." She imitated her grandmother's voice and smiled. "You're right. We can't change

unpleasant facts, so no point in crying about it."
Her shoulders fell.

Mew-Maw took her hand and led her to the
swing. "Yeah, well, we've seen how well that
philosophy worked with my daughter. I thought
we agreed to do things differently. What did that
boy do to break your heart? I can lock him up
with Brutus. That's one mean bull."

Lyrissa laughed. It was a little dry, but more
than she thought she was capable of today. "No
one deserves that, Mew-Maw. Knowing Reno,
he'd have him eating from the palm of his hand.
I thought you were going to sell that old bull."

"I have a soft spot for that old man. I'm afraid
no one else would put up with him. We suit each
other just fine." She squeezed Lyrissa's hand.
"Tell me what our boy has done."

She shrugged. "I think he loves me."

Her grandmother blinked at her. "Not what I
was expecting. His mother called, worried." Her
words were slow and measured, as if she was
dealing with a skittish foal. "She saw you leave,
upset. When she tried to talk to Reno, he wasn't
himself. She was worried about you. Men can be
clueless when it comes to matters of the heart."

Lyrissa snorted. "I'm pretty sure the women
of our family are heartless."

Mew-Maw narrowed her wrinkled eyes.
"I'm…"

She leaned into her grandmother and hugged her. "I'm sorry. I'm all out of sorts, but there was no excuse for that. We just don't deal with emotions well."

With a sigh, her grandmother hugged her. "That might be an understatement of the century. I'm so sorry I passed this on to you and your mother."

Tears dampened her shirt. She sat up and stared at her grandmother. "Are you crying?"

The older woman wiped at her face. "Don't be silly. Of course I'm not crying."

Lyrissa caressed her thumb over the work-worn, beautifully wrinkled skin. "It's okay to cry. We're a mess. Reno wanted to start dating. I told him there was no future for us. I can't bring him into this family. I don't think I can love someone the way he deserves to be loved. I don't trust myself or him to not get hurt beyond repair. I mean, look at my parents. I just can't risk that with someone who's so good."

"Oh, baby girl. You're not your mother or your father. Or any other member of your family. Our blood may run through your veins, but you are a child of God first and foremost. You're Lyrissa Herff Martinez. Do you have faith in Him?"

"To be honest, I'm not sure. A month ago, I would have said yes, but I wasn't living in that faith. Now I'm on rocky ground. I want to trust

God with everything, but I have certain bits I know I'm holding back on."

"You can't allow your parents' drama to derail you from God's plan. Take hold of your faith and trust in God. Without it, what's the point of life? We can't control what happens to us or the people around us, but we can control our reactions."

"Reno has asked me to trust him."

"Do you?"

Lyrissa shrugged.

"I've known Reno for most of his life. More so as an adult. He's a good man. If you don't love him, then you're doing the right thing. But I fear you do love him and you're walking away from the one man who you can build a real life with. Someone who will stand by your side."

"How do I know which it is?"

"Deep inside, you know. God does not lead with fear. Be still and listen. That's why I ride out so much now, even when I don't need to. I'm so busy making plans and having opinions, I have a tough time listening."

Lyrissa pulled her knees to her chest and rested her head on her grandmother's chest. The older woman gathered the quilt over their shoulders. The love of past generations surrounded them.

"I love him," she whispered.

Mew-Maw nodded. "Then you go get him and let him know."

"What if I'm too late?"

"I don't believe you are."

Lyrissa thought about the note Reno had given to her the day in the hospital. He didn't know he had asked her to marry him, but she had a feeling he had meant it.

Did he still see her in his long-term future? There was so much uncertainty. But together, they would figure it out. First, she had to open up and be honest with him.

The thought of laying all of her heart out in front of him made her a little sick to her stomach. "I don't know if I can do it."

"If you start, I think he will meet you halfway. If he doesn't and you find yourself standing alone, then it's not meant to be. But you will never know if you don't take that first step and reach out to him."

She had to find a way to prove to him that she was in this for the long haul. He had every reason to doubt her. How many times had he stepped closer, only for her to run away?

She got her phone out and texted him. Can we meet tomorrow after work?

No, I've got the test. I'm turning my phone off. Night.

Blinking, she stared at the phone. He had never cut her off like that. Was she too late? *No.* He was stressed over the exam, and she would only make it worse. She would back off and let him focus.

What she needed was a plan to prove she was ready for a relationship with him. And she could handle the uncertainty of a future as long as he was in her life.

Together they could get through anything. She knew that without a doubt. She loved him and he deserved to know that.

Sending one more text, she smiled. Now to make plans and trust God had them.

Reno double-checked the time then the message. 5:00 p.m. at the barns.

I am in the right place at the right time. But the wrong guy again.

Why was he here? He had made a promise to himself not to let her tie him in knots. Her happiness was all he wanted. Of course, in a perfect world it would be with him.

The horse reached for him out of the half door. He rubbed her muzzle. "I think I lied when I thought we could still be friends." He loved Lyrissa more than he thought possible. Too much to just sit on the bench.

Stepping out of the barn, he scanned the area.

What if there was a problem? Fists stuffed into his jeans, he bit his lip. What if there was trouble and he had cut her off?

Sunday night, in an angry fit he had turned his phone off. The test had to have his full focus. As soon as his test was over, he stepped outside and turned his phone on. Seeing all the missed calls had dropped his stomach. But the last text had given him hope. You've got this. Meet me at the barn Tuesday at 5:00 p.m. I have something I want to show you.

Was he at the right barn? What if something was wrong? She hadn't returned any calls or his text in the last hour. He blew out a puff of air. He should have come out to the ranch earlier.

Should he send another message letting her know he was here? Had she changed her mind?

After another long breath in, he went back into the barn. "Looks like she stood me up again, Cinnamon." He rubbed the horse's soft muzzle. He'd check at the house then head home.

He turned to the door then froze. Lyrissa stood there. One hand pressed against the frame. Each breath came hard and heavy and her hair was a mess.

A canvas saddlebag was thrown over her shoulder. "Oh good. You're still here. We had an issue at school. Then on the way home I went to call you. Realized my phone was dead. And my cord—" she took another breath "—wasn't charging."

All doubts left, replaced by concern. He moved to her, his hand lifted to her face. He searched her eyes. "Are you okay?"

Standing, she nodded. "Yes. I had a big plan to…" She waved a hand in the air. "Well. I was hoping to show you something. Do you feel like a ride?"

He shook his head to clear his thoughts. "That was a huge change of subject." Why was she acting like their last conversation never happened? "I'm always up for a ride. But Lyrissa, I'm confused. The last time we talked, you made it clear you couldn't be more than friends. I know you've counted on my friendship but I'm still a little raw. So, what's this all about?"

She bit her lip. "I know I've been the queen of mixed signals, and you did put yourself out there, only to get rejected. I'm sorry I didn't respond the way I should have. I let fear rule me, but I want a redo. Can we do that? Will you give me the chance to start over? I can't lose your friendship or you." She stood before him, her big eyes shining and asking him for another chance.

And he crumbled. He nodded. "Of course. There's a secret you haven't learned yet. With me, you will always have another chance. I'm not going anywhere."

She smiled, but there was a suspicious glint of moisture in her eyes. "Good. No more talking. Let's get the horses saddled."

It didn't take them long to be on horseback. She pointed her horse to the west, and he followed. They made their way across her family ranch, following a narrow path through the knee-high grass. The creaking of the saddle and the thumping of hooves on packed dirt were the only sounds.

His heart fell into rhythm with his horse and the stress slipped away with each sway. The sun was still high above the horizon and birds glided on the wind. There were enough clouds to break the sun's intensity. They came to a gate, and she opened it with a well-practiced side step.

"We're leaving your ranch?" he asked in surprise.

"Yes. I found this old path as a teenager. I didn't want anyone to tell me not to come this way. So, I kept it a secret." She smiled at him, the kind that made her eyes sparkle. "I'm sharing my best-kept secret with you."

A pair of huge cranes lifted themselves into the sky. A small herd of Angus cows grazed in the distance. Tall, golden grass gently rustled in the breeze.

They followed an overgrown path up a small hill. At the top, the view before him took his breath away. The Gulf of Mexico reached as far from the east as to the west. Billowing clouds hovered over the horizon where the water touched the sky.

"Lyrissa, this is breathtaking." It was a place of peace. He felt it seep into his bones and banished his last worries.

"It's my favorite place in the world and I've never told anyone about it. Let alone shared it." She dismounted and pulled the rolled blanket off the back of her saddle and untied the bag.

Stopping about five feet from the edge of the cliff, she spread a blanket over the ground. She went back to her saddlebag. "I have a few things to eat and two bottles of water."

Worry was stamped in her beautiful eyes when she finally made eye contact with him. "I've been planning for this since Sunday night. I don't want you to be mad at me. Your friendship is so important."

The rigidity was back in his muscles. All peace was gone with one word. When had he started hating the word *friend*? She sat down and patted the space next to her. "Join me."

The horizon held all his attention. Otherwise, he might start yelling at her to stop sitting there looking all innocent and sweet. She had torn out his heart and it still hurt. He knew himself enough that if he said what he wanted without a filter, the guilt would eat him alive. So, he bit the inside of his mouth and prayed as he stared at the clouds shifting and changing with the wind.

He should just go along and pretend everything was fine. That way, when he had gotten over himself, they would still be friends.

"Reno. Please talk to me. Don't pretend everything is okay if it's not. Not with me."

She was right. He respected her too much to give her the same old song and dance. He couldn't sit, though. Not yet. Gaze still fixed on the moving clouds, he took a deep breath. No matter how much pain he was in, the world would keep going. That was a truth he had learned long ago. "I'm tired of being the guy who's always easygoing and fun."

Dropping his gaze, he studied the ground and stuffed his hands in his pockets.

"You are so much more than that guy. Reno, I brought you here to talk to you about our future. I can't see mine without you in it."

As a friend. He shook his head. "I can't do this. I told you that I loved you and I want to build a family with you. You said no and left. Today, I can't go back to just being your friend. Not yet. Give me some time and I'm sure I'll get over it."

There was movement behind him. In less than a minute, she stood next to him, but he couldn't look at her. His deepest feelings were raw and exposed.

He tilted his head back and looked at the endless sky above them. *God, I could really use some help here. A bit of wisdom or something. I'm not even sure what I'm asking for.*

She slid her hand along his forearm and pulled until her fingers were wrapped with his. "Reno, I didn't bring you out here just to talk and hang out and tell you about all my troubles. We've done a lot of that, and you've been there for me through so much upheaval. I also want to be there for you. I know you have your family, but I don't think you really allow them to see you. I want to be your safe space."

She stepped back and pulled something out of her pocket. She took a deep breath and looked down at the piece of paper, then up at him.

"Sit down with me, please." She pulled her bottom lip between her teeth and just looked at him with those huge, soft eyes.

He sighed. With a nod, he moved to her blanket. He'd give her anything. "Okay." He dropped to the green-and-red plaid.

She sat across from him. "I want to give something back to you." She had the paper in her hand. It was torn off from a larger piece. "This is what you gave me in the hospital."

His stomach twisted and his heart pounded faster. "When I was basically unconscious."

She laughed. "You were conscious. You just didn't have your filters in place." She reached out to him. "I want to give it back to you with an answer."

Swallowing, he took the paper from her and with complete dread, looked down. Yeah, it was his writing. This was so humiliating. He looked at the uneven scrawl of letters. It wasn't bad for a first grader just learning to write. Each letter was wonky but bold. All caps. *WIL U MARY M.* There was a mark after the *m* that he supposed was an *e* but it looked more like a *z*.

He had asked her to marry him. In this crude, primitive writing. He blinked.

On the bottom, evenly slanted letters spaced carefully apart read *Let's date, then ask me again*. He couldn't breathe.

"Reno. I would have said yes, but you weren't in your right mind. So, I thought it only fair to give you time to reconsider the question."

"Do you have a pencil?" He was floating, maybe even flying right off the cliff, and gliding over the ocean.

Stay focused, Bucko. He could hear his dad's voice. His eyes burned at the thought that his dad was here, encouraging and guiding him.

"Are you okay? You read that, right?" There was a nervous edginess to her voice.

He smiled, trying to keep it cool. He doubted he was successful. "You always have pencils or pens or something to write with. Do you have one with you now?"

She stood. "I think so." She wasn't gone long, then came back and sank to her knees. "Here."

He turned the paper over. Very carefully, he wrote the question again. *Lyrissa, will you marry me?*

He looked up. Curiosity and uncertainty along with hope and joy warred on her lovely face.

He cleared his throat. "Before I give this back to you, I should tell you I love you, with all my heart, body and mind. You are my home, and I would love to date you for the rest of my life." He handed the note back to her.

For the longest minute she started at the note. It was cupped in both her hands as if it was the most precious gift. After a heartbeat or two she pulled it to her chest and looked up at him. "I'm so sorry I responded in fear the other day." She took a breath. "Yes. Reno, I love you and would love to be your wife."

The wind came up over the cliff and swirled around them. A bird called out. He pulled her close and kissed her without trepidation or fear. She wrapped her arms around him.

He rested his forehead against hers. "Can we stay here forever? Right here?"

With a laugh, she shook her head. "I don't want to miss the rest of our lives. I love you, Reno."

Before he could respond, his phone vibrated. The world was already intruding. He glanced down. "It's the fire chief. They said they would let us know today."

He hesitated. Did he want to know right now?

She put her hand over his. "It doesn't matter what the results are. You're so talented. If you don't become a firefighter, there are other paths for you. You'll find the right one. And I'll be by your side."

"If I passed then I'd have to stay here. Go through the training. We can live in Port Del Mar or over the bridge. I'm so—"

She shook her head. "No. I've already decided to take the job here. I need to stay close to my family. Mom is so unpredictable. I would be so worried if I wasn't here for them."

He looked down at his phone with a frown. "Oh no. I waited too long. The call ended."

"Call back." Her smile lit up her eyes. "No matter the news, we've got this. God has a plan if we take the time to listen and not react with fear or pride. I just figured it out. I'm sure you'll have to remind me a few times."

He hit the number and called. "It's Reno. I missed your call."

"Well, son. It is an honor and my privilege to welcome you to…"

Reno didn't hear the rest of the words. He might have blacked out. His dream had just come true. He glanced at Lyrissa, her face blank as she tried to read his expression.

He smiled and she smiled back.

"Yes, sir. I'll see you Monday." He hoped that had been the correct response. His brain was buzzing.

Once he put the phone down, she leaped across the space between them and hugged him tight, knocking him back. "You did it."

"*We* did it. I have a feeling together we can do anything we want."

"I love you and trust you with my heart and my future, Fireman Reno Espinoza."

After kissing her, he pressed his lips against her ear. "Forever and ever. Amen."

Epilogue

He glanced at his watch. Where had everyone gone? He was supposed to be getting married in less than twenty minutes and his best man and little groomsmen were missing in action. His stomach fluttered but not in nervousness. Lyrissa was about to become his wife.

If everything was okay. Okay, so he was a little nervous. He glanced around the study of the old ranch house, searching for his phone. This room was fancier than anything he'd ever been in. From here they would be driving up to Lyrissa's favorite spot.

The Wimberlys owned the largest ranch in the area. They were gracious enough to not only let them get married on the property, but gave the use of their home to get ready in and provided shuttles up to the lookout point. Somewhere in the other side of the large house, Lyrissa was with her parents getting ready. One of her friends from college was standing with her. Her mother had been home for a few months and things had been going well. Mundo and she were even talking about a recommitment ceremony. But maybe she did something.

Lyrissa, the boys, Mundo and Edith—his new family—would all be devastated.

He went across the room to get his phone. The heavy oak door opened, and his tiny mother slipped into the room. His heart slammed against his chest. Had she come to tell him something had gone wrong? "Is it Dee?"

"What? Oh, no. Everyone is good." The smile on her face calmed him. "Oh *mijo*, you're so handsome. Of all my children, you look the most like your father." She cut across the room and cupped his face. "I'm so proud of you."

"Thank you, *mami*."

"You saved me, you know? All of my kids did. In one way or another. But you, my baby, gave me a reason to get out of bed every morning. Your smile and laughter brought me so much joy in my darkest days. But I never meant for you to take on that responsibility and carry it by yourself. I'm so sorry for that. Please tell me you've released that burden."

He hugged her. "I'll always do whatever to make my mother happy. But, yes, I'm good. In another hour I'll be even better. Do you know where Bridges and the boys are?"

Bennett and Ray-Ray had been so proud and excited to be his groomsmen. They were going to spend the day with Lyrissa. She was going to make sure they were ready then send them over. "The boys should've been here by now."

"They're on the way. I asked for a few minutes alone with you."

"Oh? Is that why Bridges suddenly had something he had to take care of?"

The extra twinkle in her eyes warned him she was up to something.

"*Mami*, what is going on?"

Instead of answering, she opened her little purse and pulled out a box. "I have something I promised your father I would give you on a special day." She looked up at him, unshed tears hovering in her eyes. "I think today is it."

His throat went dry as she opened the lid and pulled out an old-fashioned wristwatch with a leather band. "That's Dad's watch. Shouldn't it be given to Bridges?"

She shook her head. "When you were five all you wanted was a watch like your dad's. And Bridges loves those fancy smartwatches with his heart rate and steps. But you always wanted this watch. Your dad knew that and asked me to save it for you. And to make sure you knew he'd always be with you. Here."

She held out her hand. "Let me take your old watch off and put on your father's."

His throat was tight as she removed his watch and set it to the side. They stood in silence as she put his father's watch on his wrist. She patted it. "It belongs here."

Unable to talk, he pulled her into his arms. For a long moment they stood there. He took a deep breath. "Thank you. On the day I asked Lyrissa to marry me, I heard his voice."

She stepped back and cupped his face. "Of course you did." She laid her hand flat against his heart. "He's always here."

The door swung open with a lot of energy. Bennett and Ray-Ray burst into the room. "We're here to distract you!" Ray-Ray yelled.

"Distract me?" He grinned.

Bennett hit his little brother on the shoulder. "We're not supposed to tell him that."

He looked at his mother. "What's going on?"

She shrugged with a mischievous grin. "I have no idea. But I have something I need to take care of. Just a heads-up we will be late. So don't worry. Lyrissa is ready. There is just one detail. When I come back, we'll be riding up to the spot. Love you." And she was gone.

He looked at his new little brothers. "What's going on, guys? Is your sister okay?"

Ray-Ray bit his lip and gave a side-glance to

his brother. Bennett tilted his head, avoiding any eye contact. "Uhm. Everything's good. There's a surprise, and we were told not to tell you be-cause…it's a surprise."

His mind raced. What kind of surprise would make everyone late?

"Lyrissa said you had pizza." Bennett moved to the table and lifted a lid off a pizza box.

"Freeze! Let's slip a T-shirt over your tux-edo. Your sister will kill me if you get sauce on your fancy duds." He found his shirt and one of Bridges's and covered the boys.

They had devoured one of the pizzas when a slight knock drew their attention. "Come in."

Was this the surprise? The door eased open. He froze, not believing what he saw. Savannah, his sister, stepped into the room. She had been gone so long, without a word. All he had known was his sister and best friend had disappeared from his life for the safety of her new family.

"Savannah?" She wore a pretty sage-green dress, and her dark hair was pulled up with curls falling around her face. She was also very preg-nant.

"Hey, baby brother. I hear congratulations are in order."

He rushed her and lifted her into a hug. Well, he tried. Her belly was in the way. "Sorry. Wow.

There's so much to talk about. What are you doing here? Is it safe?"

"I called Momma yesterday to let her know the threat to Greyson and the girls was over and we planned to move back home. I want to have our baby boy here. She told me you were getting married."

"A boy? That's great. We can use a few more boys in this family." He shook his head. "I can't believe you're here."

"There's no way I would miss the wedding of my little brother and best friend." She squeezed his shoulder. "Really? Lyrissa? I can't believe you're marrying her. I knew you always had a thing for her. Later, you're going to have to tell me how this all happened. And I can get you caught up with my life. Now introduce me to these fine young men."

He cleaned them up and removed the shirts as he introduced them to his sister. The door opened and his brother and mother came into the room. "Okay. Okay. More talking later. We have a wedding to get to," his mother announced.

He hugged Savannah one more time before she left to join his soon-to-be bride.

Bridges gripped his shoulder. "We have a Jeep at the side of the house. Once we head out, Lyrissa and her party will follow in a few minutes. Ready to get married, little brother?"

Bennett and Ray-Ray cheered, "Yes!"

Reno wasn't sure he needed the Jeep. It was as if he could float all the way to the spot where she had first told him she loved him.

Chairs had been set up and were filled with people. Pastor Rod stood under a wooden archway covered with greenery and flowers.

The light faded into soft pinks and blues at the horizon, just like the day that changed his life. He walked down the aisle with his mother on his arm. His older brother and two little brothers followed.

With a kiss on her cheek, he sat his mother down in the front row with his sisters. They were all smiling like fools. Then he stood and waited.

When she first came into view, he lost his breath. His Lyrissa was a princess in a white gown. The top was simple and fitted to her but then flared out a little. The skirt was covered in lace flowers.

Music came from somewhere, but he only saw her. Pastor Rod spoke but he just looked into the eyes of the woman he loved. He promised to love, honor and cherish her and slipped her ring onto her finger. She was his. He was hers.

It was over and they turned to face everyone. But he couldn't take his gaze off her. They walked to the Jeep that would take them to the Painted Dolphin to celebrate their wedding.

Bridges drove and they slipped into the back seat.

She cupped his face and kissed him. "It's official. I'm yours."

"And I belong to you, completely." He pressed his forehead to hers and soaked up her presence. The good and the bad ahead of them would be better because she was by his side.

* * * * *

If you liked this story from Jolene Navarro, check out her previous Love Inspired books:

The Reluctant Rancher
Bound by a Secret
Claiming Her Texas Family

Available now from Love Inspired!
Find more great reads at
www.LoveInspired.com.

Dear Reader,

Thank you for taking this trip to Port Del Mar with me. This is my twelfth book set in this fictional town and it has become very real to me. Exploring small towns and ranch life along the Texas coast has been fun.

Reno has been hanging out with me for four books. I knew he needed someone to come in and see past his charming smile. Of all my people, he and Lyrissa are drawn the most from my real-life experiences. I went through school undiagnosed also. It wasn't until college I discovered what dysgraphia was. I went on to earn my Masters in Special Ed with a specialty in reading.

My husband was Reno's Lyrissa. With his support and my faith in God I stepped out and dared to tell stories of people overcoming. It has been a true blessing and I pray you enjoyed reading Reno and Lyrissa's story.

Jolene Navarro

https://jolenenavarro.com/

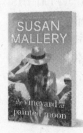